Bodyguard Under the Mistletoe

CASSIE MILES

MILLS & BOON®

First published in Great Britain 2010
Large Print edition 2010
Harlequin Mills & Boon Limited,
Eton House, 18-24 Paradise Road,
Richmond, Surrey TW9 1SR

© Kay Bergstrom 2009

ISBN: 978 0 263 21593 9

Printed and bound in Great Britain
by CPI Antony Rowe, Chippenham, Wiltshire

CASSIE MILES

Though born in Chicago and raised in L.A., Cassie Miles has lived in Colorado long enough to be considered a semi-native. The first home she owned was a log cabin in the mountains overlooking Elk Creek with a thirty-mile commute to her work at the *Denver Post*.

After raising two daughters and cooking tons of macaroni and cheese for her family, Cassie is trying to be more adventurous with her culinary efforts. Ceviche anyone? She's discovered that almost anything tastes better with wine. A lot of wine. When she's not plotting Intrigue books, Cassie likes to hang out at the Denver Botanical Gardens near her high-rise home.

To Rick.
I thought about you a lot
when I was writing this book.

Chapter One

He wasn't dead yet.

The darkness behind his eyelids thinned. Sensation prickled the hairs on his arm. Inside his head, he heard the beat of his heart—as loud and steady as the Ghost Dance drum. That sacred rhythm called him back to life.

His ears picked up other sounds. The *beep-beep-beep* of a monitor. The shuffle of quiet footsteps. The creaking of a chair. A cough. Someone else was in the room with him.

The drumming accelerated.

His eyelids opened—just a slit. Sunlight through the window blinds reflected off the white sheet that covered his prone body. Hospital equipment surrounded the bed. Oxygen. An IV drip on a metal pole. A heart monitor that beeped. Faster. Faster. Faster.

"Jesse?" A deep voice called to him. "Jesse, are you awake?"

Jesse Longbridge tried to move, tried to respond. Pain radiated from his left shoulder. He remembered being shot, falling from his saddle to the cold earth and lying there, helpless. He remembered a gush of blood. He remembered…

"Come on, Jesse. Open your eyes."

He recognized the voice of Bill Wentworth. A friend. A coworker. *Good old Wentworth.* He'd been a paramedic in Iraq, but that wasn't the main reason Jesse had hired him. This lean, mean former marine—like Jesse himself—always got the job done.

They had a mission, he and Wentworth. No

time to waste. They needed to get into the field, needed to protect…

Jesse bolted upright on the bed and gripped Wentworth's arm. "Is she safe?"

"You're awake." Wentworth grinned without showing his teeth. "It's about time."

One of the monitor wires detached, and the beeping became a high-pitched whine. "Is Nicole safe?"

"She's all right. Arrests have been made."

Wentworth was one of Jesse's best employees—a credit to Longbridge Security, an outstanding bodyguard. But he wasn't much of a liar.

The pain in his shoulder spiked again, threatening to drag Jesse back into peaceful unconsciousness. He licked his lips. His mouth was parched. He needed water. More than that, he needed the truth. He knew that Nicole had been kidnapped. He'd seen it happen. He'd been shot trying to protect her.

He tightened his grip on Wentworth's arm. "Has Nicole Carlisle been safely returned to her husband?"

"No."

Dylan Carlisle had hired Longbridge Security to protect his family and to keep his cattle ranch safe. If his wife was missing, they'd failed. Jesse had failed.

He released Wentworth. Using his right hand, he detached the nasal cannula that had been feeding oxygen to his lungs. Rubbing the bridge of his nose, he felt the bump where it had been broken a long time ago in a school-yard fight. He hadn't given up then. Wouldn't give up now. "I'm out of here."

Two nurses rushed into the room. While one of them turned off the screeching monitor, the other shoved Wentworth aside and stood by the bed. "You're wide-awake. That's wonderful."

"Ready to leave," Jesse said.

"Oh, I don't think so. You've been pretty much unconscious for three days and—"

"What's the date?"

"It's Tuesday morning. December ninth," she said.

Nicole had been kidnapped on the prior Friday, near dusk. "Was I in a coma?"

"After surgery, your brain activity stabilized. You've been consistently responsive to external stimuli."

"I'll say," Wentworth muttered. "When a lab tech tried to draw blood, you woke up long enough to grab him by the throat and shove him down on his butt."

"I didn't hurt him, did I?"

"He's fine," the nurse said, "but you're not his favorite patient."

He didn't belong in a hospital. Three days was long enough for recuperation. "I want my clothes."

The nurse scowled. "I know you're in pain."

Nothing he couldn't handle. "Are you going to take these needles out of my arms or should I pull them myself?"

She glanced toward Wentworth. "Is he always this difficult?"

"Always."

FIONA GRANT PLACED a polished, rectangular oak box on her kitchen table and lifted the lid. Inside, nestled in red velvet, was a pearl-handled, antique Colt .45 revolver.

In her husband's will, he'd left this heirloom to Jesse Longbridge, and Fiona didn't begrudge his legacy. She'd tried to arrange a meeting with Jesse to present this gift, but their schedules had gotten in the way. After her husband's death, she hadn't been efficient in handling the myriad details, and she hoped Jesse would understand. She was eternally grateful to the bodyguard who had saved her husband's life. Because of Jesse's quick actions, she'd gained a few more precious years with her darling Wyatt before he died from a heart attack at age forty-eight.

People always said she was too young to be a widow. Not even thirty when Wyatt died. Now thirty-two. Too young? As if there was an acceptable age for widowhood? As if her daughter—now four years old—would have been better off losing her dad when she was ten? Or fifteen? Or twenty?

Age made no difference. Fiona hadn't been bothered by the age disparity between Wyatt and herself when they married. All she knew was that she had loved her husband with all her heart. And so she was thankful to Jesse Longbridge. She fully intended to hand over the gun to him when he got out of the hospital. In the meantime, she didn't think he'd mind if she used it.

Her fingertips tentatively touched the cold metal barrel and recoiled. She didn't like guns, but owning one was prudent—almost mandatory for ranchers in western Colorado. Not that Fiona considered herself a rancher. Her hundred-acre property was tiny compared to the neighboring Carlisle empire that had over two thousand head of Black Angus. She had no livestock, even though her daughter, Abby, kept telling her that she really, really, really wanted a pony.

Fiona frowned at the gun. *Who am I kidding? I'm not someone who can handle a Colt .45.* She turned, paced and paused. Stared through the window above the sink. The view of distant snow-covered peaks, pine forests and the faded yellow grasses of winter pastures failed to calm her jangled nerves.

For the past three days, a terrible kidnapping drama had been playing out at the Carlisle Ranch. Their usually pastoral valley had been invaded by posses, FBI agents, search helicopters and bloodhounds that sniffed their way right up to her front doorstep.

Last night, people were taken into custody.

The danger should have been over. But just after two o'clock last night, Fiona had heard voices outside her house. She hadn't been able to tell how close they were and hadn't seen the men. But they were loud and angry, then suddenly silent.

The quiet that followed their argument had frightened her more than the shouts. What if they came to her door? Could she stop them if they tried to break in? The sheriff was twenty miles away. If she'd called the Carlisle Ranch, someone would come running. But would they arrive in time?

The truth had dawned with awful clarity. She and Abby had no one to protect them. Their safety was her responsibility.

Hence, the gun.

Returning to the kitchen table, she stared at it. She never expected to be alone, never expected to be living in this rustic log house on a full-time basis. This was a vacation home—

a place where she and Abby and Wyatt spent time in the summer so her husband could unwind from his high-stress job as Denver's district attorney.

Water under the bridge. She was here now. This was her home, and she needed to be able to defend it.

She lifted the Colt from the case, surprised by how heavy it felt when she supported it with one hand. The lethal weapon seemed foreign in her cheerful kitchen with its tangerine walls and Abby's crayon artwork decorating the refrigerator.

It was a good thing that her daughter was with the babysitter in town. She didn't want to frighten the child. Or, more likely, send her into gales of laughter at the sight of her mousy, pottery-making mother acting tough.

Peering down the long barrel, Fiona aimed at the toaster on the counter. She snarled, "Go ahead. Make my day."

The toaster didn't back down.

Through the kitchen window, she saw a figure on horseback approaching the rear of the house. Carolyn Carlisle.

Quickly, Fiona tucked the antique gun back into its case and placed it on top of the refrigerator. She grabbed a green corduroy jacket from a peg by the back door. Thrusting her arms into the sleeves, she pulled her long brown braid out from the collar and went down the steps into the yard.

After a skillful dismount, Carolyn met her with a quick hug. A tall woman with her black hair pulled back in a ponytail under her cowboy hat, Carolyn looked comfortable in boots, jeans and a black shearling vest.

Though Fiona had grown up near San Francisco, she loved Western outfits, except for the boots. They squeezed her toes. She preferred sandals. Or the sneakers she was wearing today.

"Good news," Carolyn said. "Jesse Longbridge is awake. He's expected to make a full recovery."

"That's a relief."

"I don't know if my brother ever thanked you for recommending Longbridge Security. Jesse and his men have been more than competent."

Fiona wasn't surprised. Her husband always said Longbridge Security was the best. "What about Nicole?"

"We've heard from her. She says she's okay, and we shouldn't worry."

"But she's still not home?"

"Things didn't work out the way they should have."

Fiona's heart went out to her neighbor. "I'm sorry."

"I have no intention of leaving things this way. My brother's sulking around like a whipped puppy. We lost a million-dollar ransom. And I won't believe Nicole's all right until I hear the words from her own lips."

Her hand fisted. "I'm not done yet. Not by a long shot."

Fiona wished she had one-tenth of Carolyn's determination. When she wasn't at the ranch, Carolyn was a hard-driving businesswoman, the CEO of Carlisle Certified Organic Beef—an international, multimillion-dollar business.

"Would you like to come inside?" Fiona asked. "Have a cup of coffee?"

"Not necessary."

Fiona moved closer to Carolyn's horse. Elvis was a big handsome mahogany brown stallion with a black mane and a white blaze on his forehead. She glided her hand along his bristly coat. Gently, she encouraged her friend to open up. "I heard that the kidnappers were arrested."

"The FBI closed down that survivalist group that was staying at the Circle M Ranch. Nicole wasn't there."

"You said she called last night."

"It's crazy. I don't even know where to start."

While Fiona waited for Carolyn to sort out her thoughts, she continued to pet the horse. Elvis ducked his head and bared his teeth in a horsey grin. "Is he flirting with me?"

"Elvis is shameless, but don't give him anything to eat. The last thing I need is a fat Elvis."

Fiona chuckled, but Carolyn didn't crack a smile. She was so tightly wound that Fiona thought she might start spinning like a top. Apparently, she wasn't ready to continue with her story because she changed the topic. "I haven't even asked about you, Fiona. How's Abby?"

"She's fine. Right now she's with the babysitter in Riverton."

"You're not usually at your cabin in December."

Not wanting to launch into a dissertation about her own problems, Fiona looked up at the cloudless blue sky. "The weather's been amazing. Almost as warm as Denver. Do you think we'll have a white Christmas?"

"Christmas is Nicole's favorite time of year." Her voice cracked. "She decorates like mad. I don't know how to do any of that stuff."

"I'll help," Fiona offered. "Let's walk while we talk."

With Elvis following behind them, they made their way across the dry winter grass, skirting the edge of the lodgepole and ponderosa pines that formed a natural barrier around Fiona's house. Her rocky, forested land had never been intended for farming or grazing.

"Before Nicole was abducted," Carolyn said, "she and my brother had an argument. Last night, when they met face-to-face, she told him that the kidnapping gave her time to think, and she decided not to come home. She never wants to see Dylan again."

"She wants a divorce?"

"Apparently." Carolyn kicked a pinecone from

her path. "Dylan won't talk to me. Or anybody else. Whatever Nicole said, it was enough to convince him. He called off the search."

"Can he do that?" No matter what the victim said, kidnapping was still a crime. "Isn't the FBI involved?"

"The FBI profilers and search teams were willing to back off. They blame Nicole's behavior on Stockholm syndrome."

"They think Nicole fell in love with her captor?"

"I don't believe it. Nicole and my brother are soul mates. Damn it, she wouldn't leave him. Not like that." Carolyn's determination flared. "I'm not letting this investigation die. I convinced one of the FBI agents to stay. Even if my brother doesn't like it."

She stopped walking. They stood at a high point on a ridge, looking down at the barbed-wire fence that separated their property. In a pasture near the trees, a large herd of cattle were grazing. A field of improbably green winter wheat, planted in late September, stretched out to the road.

Fiona loved this view—a patchwork of subtle winter colors punctuated by the green of the wheat and the heavy black shapes of cattle.

Elvis stepped up beside her and nudged her shoulder like an oversize dog who wanted to be petted. She stroked his neck. "If Nicole is with her kidnapper, that means he's still at large. Right?"

"There are two of them. One of them has a criminal record as long as your arm. The other is Butch Thurgood—supposedly the guy Nicole likes. He's won top prizes in rodeos for bronc busting, and he has a reputation for being a horse whisperer."

"Last night," Fiona said, "I heard two men arguing. I didn't see them, but they were close to my house."

"Did you search?"

Fiona shook her head. It had never occurred

to her to go poking around in the dark. "Do you think it was them?"

"It's worth investigating. I'll tell Burke, and we'll come back over here."

"Burke?"

"The FBI agent who stayed behind." When she said his name, her features relaxed. "Can I ask you something? Woman to woman."

"Okay."

"How did you know? When you met Wyatt, how did you know he was the man you wanted to spend the rest of your life with?"

"It's not something I planned for. My heart told me."

"Lucky you." Carolyn gave a wry grin. "My heart isn't so direct. I'd know what to do about Burke if I could refer to a balance sheet or see a prospectus."

Though Fiona respected her neighbor's keen business sense and focus, she didn't believe these denials. "It's obvious that you care about him. Even if it doesn't make rational sense, you might even love him."

"I've been in love before, and it hasn't worked."

"You'll never know what's going to happen with Burke unless you give it a try."

"Oh, hell. I couldn't possibly pick a more inconvenient time for this to happen." She stuck the toe of her boot into the stirrup and mounted Elvis. "I'll be back with Burke to investigate your mysterious voices in the night."

"I can't wait to meet him."

Fiona watched as Carolyn rode down the ridge to the road where she wouldn't encounter any barbed wire. Though they were the same age, Fiona felt much older. She'd already been through her own cycle of life—marriage, childbirth and the death of her husband.

Now she was alone again. Starting over. She envied the glow of first love that flushed Carolyn's face when she spoke of the FBI agent. Someday, she hoped to feel that way again. She remembered the sudden rush of emotion that came with love. The shivers. The heat. Hot and cold at the same time.

Instead of walking directly back to the house, she climbed the ridge. From a vantage point behind a boulder, she looked down at her property.

A cool December wind shook the branches of the pines. In spite of the bright sunlight pouring down, she shivered. The voices she had heard last night could have been coming from the barn. Or the toolshed. Or the unfinished pottery studio Wyatt had been constructing for her.

She glimpsed something moving at the back of the house. A shadow that resembled the silhouette of a man. She squinted hard, trying to be sure of the vague shape she thought she'd seen. Was someone creeping around her house?

Her back door slammed. The noise jolted through her like a shot. She hadn't locked up when she'd gone to greet Carolyn. That shadowy figure could have gone inside her house.

Chapter Two

Riding in the passenger seat of a black SUV with the Longbridge Security logo on the side, Jesse stared through the windshield at the blue Colorado sky. He was on his way to the Carlisle Ranch to put things right.

Behind the steering wheel, Wentworth sat tight-lipped and disapproving. He hadn't said a word on the drive from Delta to the small town of Riverton.

Red and green Christmas decorations were plentiful on the storefronts. An inflatable snowman stood outside the drugstore. No chance for making the real thing; the weather had been mild for December.

Wentworth pulled up at a stop sign. To their left was the only gas station in town. In front of the auto repair bay, a cowboy slammed the door on his truck and cursed.

"For the record," Wentworth muttered, "I think you should have stayed in the hospital."

"Duly noted." Jesse looked toward the gas station where the cowboy's ranting got louder. "What's going on over there?"

"That guy sounds like he's unhappy about the repair job on his truck. Not exactly in keeping with the spirit of goodwill to all."

As Jesse watched, the cowboy grabbed a tire iron and stormed toward the office. "Pull over."

"Aw, hell. I don't want to get involved in this."

Still, Wentworth swung the SUV into the gas station and parked by the pump. Longbridge Security wasn't connected with law enforcement, but Jesse felt a personal obligation to uphold public order.

A white-haired man in coveralls shuffled out of the gas station office. In his grease-stained hands, he aimed a double-barrel shotgun at the cowboy. "Take your business elsewhere," he growled. "Your truck ain't worth the rubber you leave behind on the road."

"I got no problem with you, Silas." The cowboy backed off. "Where the hell's your grandson?"

"I'm not the boy's keeper. Or his parole officer. Get off my property."

"I'm going."

As the cowboy made his prudent retreat, the old man lowered his shotgun and glared at Wentworth. "You boys got a problem?"

"No, sir."

Wentworth backed up and made a speedy exit.

"Quaint little town," Jesse said.

"The old man's a real character. Silas O'Toole.

He opens the gas station when he feels like it and charges what he thinks is right. I got a fill-up for less than twenty the other day."

"Colorful."

"I notice you didn't jump right out of the car to help. Are you feeling a little pain?"

"I'm fine."

That wasn't entirely true. He'd taken three bullets, and the left side of his body was hurting. His upper left thigh had been shot clean through. His left arm was nicked. The worst damage had been in his upper chest near the shoulder where the bullet burrowed deep through muscle and flesh, requiring surgery to remove it. He wore a sling to keep his left arm and shoulder immobilized.

He'd signed half a dozen forms releasing the Delta hospital and the doctors from liability if he croaked because of his insistence on leaving before they recommended.

"You lost a lot of blood," Wentworth said.

"Just flesh wounds. No bones broken. No internal organs harmed."

"When you were in surgery," Wentworth said, "the doc thought he lost you. You were dead for four minutes."

"I remember."

Jesse hadn't experienced his death as a white light. Instead, he saw himself as a youth on the reservation where he went to visit his grandparents. His mom—a blue-eyed woman of Irish descent—always encouraged him to stay in touch with his deceased father's Navajo heritage.

In his vision, he climbed up a crude wood ladder from the ceremonial kiva. His chest heaved as he inhaled a breath redolent with the richness of the earth and the scent of burning sage. His black hair hung past his shoulders, much longer than he wore it now.

Across the plain, he saw his grandfather, a white-haired shaman wearing a turquoise belt and holding an eagle feather.

His grandfather beckoned. But Jesse's feet were rooted to the soil. He couldn't go. Not yet. There was still something he needed to do on this earth.

"You remember dying?" Wentworth asked.

"Something like that." He adjusted the sling to fit more comfortably around the bandage and dressing near his shoulder. If his grandfather had still been alive, the old man would have given him herbs to use for healing. "Tell me what happened to Nicole."

"How much do you remember?"

Jesse thought back to the morning before she was grabbed. Her husband, Dylan, had hired Longbridge Security for surveillance and protection. There had been several incidents of sabotage on his ranch, including a fire that burned down one of the stables.

Jesse and three of his men, including Wentworth, had only been on the job a few hours when Nicole stormed out of the ranch house. Though she'd been warned not to take off by herself, she saddled up and rode across the field into the pine trees near a creek. Jesse followed on horseback.

He'd gotten close enough to see the two men who abducted her. He'd heard them say, "Dylan will pay a lot of money to get her back." And then…disaster.

If he'd moved faster, if his horse hadn't stepped on a twig, if he'd had a clean shot, he could have protected Nicole. Instead, he'd been shot.

"I remember getting back on my horse. But I didn't make it far before I fell out of the saddle. I talked to a woman."

"Carolyn Carlisle," Wentworth said. "Dylan's sister."

"Then I went unconscious. Tell me what happened next."

"The first thing? I saved your sorry ass."

"And I thank you for that."

"Wasn't easy," Wentworth said. "I slowed the bleeding, threw you in the back of a truck. One of the ranch hands—a kid named MacKenzie—drove like a NASCAR racer to get you to the hospital. Might have been the best triage I ever did as a paramedic."

"Is this your way of asking for a raise?"

Finally, Wentworth laughed. The level of tension between them dropped. "I guess you've done okay by me."

"That's good because I'm not sure who's going to hire Longbridge Security after word gets out that I let our client get kidnapped. What happened next?"

"The FBI was called in. There was a ransom demand for a million bucks. The FBI tracked down the kidnappers—a bunch of survivalists who were also smuggling. Case closed. Right?"

"Was it?"

"Hell, no."

Jesse shifted uncomfortably in his seat. With his right hand, he felt in his jacket pocket for the amber vial of prescription painkillers. "Go on."

"They couldn't find Nicole. Last night, she called her husband, met with him and told him that she wasn't coming home. She wants a divorce."

Jesse wasn't sure he understood. "I thought you said the kidnappers were arrested."

"Two are still at large."

"And the ransom?"

"Gone."

The Carlisle ranch house came into view in the distance. The property was bordered by a white slat fence. A gently curving road led to a big, two-story, whitewashed house with a veranda that stretched all the way across the front. Pine-covered foothills framed the area. Hard to believe so much turmoil had taken place in such an idyllic setting.

The drumbeat inside Jesse's head started up again. A low, hollow throb. "What else do you know?"

"That's about it," Wentworth said. "I haven't

been to the ranch house. The client instructed me to stay at the hospital. To protect you. You're the only eyewitness, and it seemed likely that the kidnappers might want you out of the way."

Jesse hadn't seen their faces well. They were wearing cowboy hats that shadowed their features. When he closed his eyes to get a mental picture, his pain intensified. He opened a vial of painkillers, tapped one out and gulped it down.

He didn't know what he'd say to Dylan. The word *sorry* sprang to mind. *Sorry I messed up and let Nicole get kidnapped. Sorry you lost a million-dollar ransom. Sorry your wife left you.*

He winced. All of a sudden, leaving the hospital seemed like a really bad idea. He wasn't ready for a confrontation. "Don't go through the gate. Take a left."

Wentworth followed his instruction. "Are we headed any place in particular?"

"I need a few minutes to think before I face Dylan."

It went without saying that Jesse wouldn't quit this job until it had reached a conclusion that satisfied both him and his client. Even if Dylan was ready to take his wife at her word, Jesse wanted confirmation from Nicole.

He turned his head and looked out the window. On the other side of a barbed-wire fence was a field of winter wheat. Still green. Even in December. "Slow down."

"What are you looking for?"

"Not sure."

He was hoping for clarity—a flash of insight that would point him in the right direction. In the skies above the field, a hawk circled. His grandfather would have called the bird an omen, a sign that Jesse should be like the hawk. He should be the hunter. Find Nicole. *Find the money.*

Wentworth stepped on the brake.

A woman was running toward the SUV. Her

green jacket matched the low grasses growing in the field. Her long brown braid flipped back and forth behind her.

She yanked open the passenger door. She was thin, delicate. Her cheeks flushed with the effort of running. Her gray eyes shone with a feverish light that made him want to look deeper.

"Your logo." She gasped. "You're Longbridge Security."

"Yes, ma'am," he said. "I'm Jesse Longbridge."

"I have your gun."

His gun? As she bent at the waist to catch her breath, he climbed down from his seat. His muscles were stiff from lying in a bed for three days, and his bandaged left leg trembled with the effort of supporting his weight as he stood in the road beside her. "What's your name?"

"Fiona Grant."

Wyatt Grant's widow. He never would have recognized this waiflike creature from the photograph her late husband kept on his desk.

Wyatt had been proud of his young bride. In that picture, Fiona was as serene as the Mona Lisa. Her long hair fell around her shoulders in shining curls. A diamond necklace glistened against her smooth olive skin. He'd been hired to protect Wyatt Grant a little over four years ago. If he recalled correctly, Fiona had been pregnant at the time and on bed rest.

When she caught her breath and looked up at him, he said, "I was sorry to hear about your husband's death. Wyatt was a good man."

"You have to come with me right away," she said with a sense of urgency. "I think the kidnappers are at my house."

"Did you see them?"

"Last night, I heard voices. And just a little while ago, I left the house and didn't lock the door. As I was coming back, it slammed."

"But you didn't actually see or hear them?"

"I saw something. A man."

"Describe him."

"It was only a fleeting glimpse. A shadow." She shuddered. Whatever she'd seen had scared her. "I'm not even sure I saw anything. And the wind could have slammed the door. I might be overreacting."

He reassured her. "You're right not to take any chances."

"Do you believe me?"

Much of what she'd said was jumbled, especially the part about having his gun. But she was obviously distressed, and she didn't strike him as being crazy. "We'll make sure your house is safe."

After losing Nicole to the kidnappers, he wouldn't take any more risks. Fiona needed his protection.

Chapter Three

Jesse shifted his thinking from speculation to action. If there really was an intruder at Fiona's house, they needed to act fast to make sure he didn't escape.

"Wentworth, call the Carlisle ranch for backup. Tell them we're heading to the Grant house." He opened the back door of the SUV for Fiona. "Climb in."

In the few moments it took to reach the turnoff to her ranch, Jesse formulated a simple plan. He and Wentworth would cover the front and back of the house, keeping the intruder trapped until backup arrived. With more manpower, they could search the house, then spread out and search the entire property.

Wentworth got off the phone. "Agent Burke and some men from the ranch are on the way."

"How long until they get here?"

"Five or ten minutes."

They drove up the packed dirt road leading to the house. Unlike the other ranches in the area, there was no fence circling Fiona's property. Her long one-story log cabin nested in a stand of aspen that would be beautiful in the fall when the leaves turned to gold. Behind the cabin, he saw a barn and a couple of outbuildings.

"Fiona, how many entrances does your house have?"

"Only front and back." Her voice was soft but not breathy. The tone reminded him of gentle notes played by a wooden flute. "But there are windows. If somebody wanted to escape, they could go out a window."

"Stay in the car, Fiona." Jesse glanced at Wentworth. "I'll take the front. You go around back. Don't enter until backup arrives."

As soon as Wentworth parked outside the detached garage, Jesse got out of the car. The adrenaline rush masked his pain. His gun felt natural in his hand. He could handle this. No problem.

Moving as quickly as he could with a bum leg, he took a position at the corner of the house beside a long, one-step, wood-plank porch covered by a shingled roof. From this position, he could see the entire front of the house and another side in case the intruder decided to exit through a window.

Leaning against the logs of the cabin, he felt his heartbeat drumming inside his head. His blood pumped hard. He was sweating. In his peripheral vision, darkness began to close in.

Not a good sign. He shook himself. *Stay awake. Stay alert.*

If Fiona's intruder was, in fact, one of the kidnappers, they were armed and dangerous. They hadn't hesitated before opening fire on him when he tried to rescue Nicole.

His knees began to weaken. Wentworth had been right. He needed more time to recuperate. *Too late to turn back now.* No way in hell would he allow himself to collapse. This was his job. His life.

When he glanced toward the car, he was surprised to see Fiona dart across the yard toward him. What the hell was she doing? Didn't she know it was dangerous? She flattened her back against the log wall beside him.

"What can I do to help?" she asked.

"You could have stayed in the car," he said dryly.

"This is my home. I need to be ready to defend it."

In different circumstances, he would have read her the riot act about why she ought to leave the business of security to professionals. But he wasn't exactly a shining example of rational behavior. Not today. Not when he'd left the hospital only an hour ago. Not when he was taking prescription painkillers. He wasn't fit for duty.

Later, he'd reprimand himself. For now, the best he could hope for was to avoid getting himself or Fiona shot.

"Stay close," he said to her.

"Are you all right?"

"Fine." *Damn it, I'm fine.*

"I've thought about you often, Jesse. I never got to thank you in person for saving my husband's life."

"You sent me flowers in a handmade vase." A strange gift for a man like him whose job meant he was seldom home. "And a note."

"Which wasn't enough. That was such a

crazy time. I was pregnant, and the doctor told me I had to stay in bed. Then I had the baby."

"Boy or girl?"

"My daughter's name is Abigail. Abby." As she spoke her child's name, her voice turned musical again. "She's with the babysitter."

As he focused on Fiona's delicate face, the dark edge of unconsciousness receded. Conversation might be what his brain needed to stay alert. "You said this cabin was your home. I thought you lived in Denver."

"Not anymore." She peeked around him to see the front door. "Shouldn't we be rushing inside or something?"

"We're waiting for backup." He didn't tell her that the idea that he could rush anywhere was just about as likely as sprouting wings and flying. "Why did you move up here?"

"Not by choice," she said. "I lost the house in Denver. And the Mercedes. And the boat. Pretty much everything, actually."

Her problems distracted him. He couldn't imagine that Wyatt Grant, a savvy attorney, would have left his widow in such bad shape. "Everything?"

"Forget it. I shouldn't have said anything." Her gaze turned downward. "I haven't told anybody."

"You can tell me," he said. "It won't go any further."

"Are bodyguards confidential? Like lawyers."

"Not in a legal sense. But I wouldn't have many clients if I started telling them their business."

"I'm not your client," she pointed out.

"As of this minute, I'm working for you. No charge. Pro bono."

"Deal." She held out her hand for him to shake before realizing that he was holding a gun in his right, and his left was in a sling. Her confusion ended with a fist bump against his left elbow.

"Now you can tell me anything," he said.

"There's not much to say, really. Wyatt had an

ex-wife, and two adult children from that marriage. They weren't happy with the terms of his will. Their attorneys froze everything that was jointly owned, including our checking and savings accounts. When I couldn't pay the bills, they swooped in. The only reason I have this cabin is that Wyatt signed the deed over to me on our first anniversary. It's in my name only."

"You must have contested the family's actions."

"Not as much as I should have. Obviously." There was an edge of bitterness in her voice. "I didn't have a taste for arguing. Nothing seemed to matter, except for my daughter. It took all my energy to crawl out of bed and take care of her."

"You let everything go." Probably even that diamond necklace she'd been wearing in the photograph.

"Didn't seem worth the effort to hold on. Not when I'd already lost the most important thing in my life."

A caravan of vehicles from the Carlisle Ranch

made the turn off the main road and poured toward them. Jesse would have liked to be the man in control; leadership was natural to him. But he was in no shape to be calling the shots.

He looked down at the slender, delicate woman who stood beside him. "I'm sorry, Fiona."

"Don't be." A mysterious Mona Lisa smile lifted the corner of her mouth. "Starting over isn't the worst thing that could happen."

Two trucks and a Jeep parked beside the Longbridge SUV. Nine or ten armed men disembarked. Through a blurry haze, Jesse watched the guy who seemed to be in charge disperse the other men to surround the house. Then he ran across the yard toward Jesse and Fiona.

"Special Agent J. D. Burke," he introduced himself. "You must be Jesse Longbridge."

"Must be." Burke was a big guy, as broadshouldered as a linebacker. Standing next to Fiona, he looked like a giant—a competent, intelligent giant. "You got here fast."

"We were already planning to come over here when Wentworth called. Carolyn mentioned that Fiona heard voices last night."

"But I haven't actually seen anyone," she piped up. "Agent Burke, you're not going to break my front door down, are you?"

"I'd rather not."

"The back is unlocked."

He gave a brisk nod. "We'll enter through the back. You both stay here and keep an eye on the front. Does that sound all right to you, Jesse?"

"It does."

He appreciated the way Burke had consulted him before taking action. Jesse wanted to think he was still capable. Like all marines, he was a sharpshooter. Even with blurred vision, he trusted his aim. "Stay behind me, Fiona. If I need to open fire, you should run to the back of the house."

"I've never done anything like this," she whispered.

"You shouldn't have to. You're a mom."

"That's exactly why I should know how to protect myself and my daughter."

From the rear of the house, he heard Burke making his entrance. Jesse's muscles tensed. He raised his handgun and stood ready to shoot.

No one came out.

After a long couple of moments, he heard Wentworth call to him, "All clear, Jesse. There's nobody in the house."

Staying focused had been a strain. His gun hand dropped to his side. He sagged against the wall. As soon as his eyes closed, darkness welled up around him. Sweet and silent. For three days, he had rested in the embrace of darkness, peaceful as a tomb.

He felt a hand against his cheek. Her touch was cool, soothing. He blinked and focused on her wide gray eyes.

"Jesse? Are you all right?"

"Fine," he mumbled.

As she studied him, her face filled with concern. Though her lips didn't move, he heard an echo of her soft voice inside his head. *Starting over isn't so bad.*

After his failure to protect Nicole, he wouldn't mind having a fresh start. A new direction for his life.

He'd been looking for a sign, a reason he had come back from death. And he sensed that Fiona might hold the answer to his deepest questions. She might provide him with a reason to go on living.

Chapter Four

Standing in her front room, Fiona wasn't sure whether she should be scared or embarrassed that she'd reported an intruder who didn't exist.

She couldn't turn to Jesse for guidance; he'd disappeared into the kitchen, moving slowly. When they were outside and he leaned against the wall with his eyes closed, she'd thought he was going to keel over, which wasn't surprising considering his injuries. Carolyn had told her that he was unconscious for three days. Jesse was still weak and ought to be in bed. Not that he'd ever admit it. Typical man! When men got sick, they either put on a macho attitude or curled up in bed and whined like babies.

Agent Burke was giving the orders. "Everybody out," he said. "We need to spread out and search."

It went against her instincts as a hostess to have these men troop through her house without offering hospitality. "I should make coffee."

"Later," Burke said.

Turning away from her, he spoke to the man who had been in the car with Jesse. Wentworth? Burke rattled off instructions about how the outbuildings should be searched and reminded him that they should proceed with caution.

Fiona could see why Carolyn had fallen for this big, rugged FBI agent. Not only was Burke a fine-looking man, but he seemed strong-willed enough to stand up to Carolyn's dynamic personality. These two would strike sparks off each other for sure.

While the searchers dispersed, she asked, "Is there something you'd like me to do, Agent Burke?"

"I'll get the sheriff over here to dust for prints, but I doubt we'll find anything. You keep a tidy house, Fiona."

"Except for the enclosed porch off the kitchen. I'm using that as my pottery studio."

"Let's take a look around and see if anything's missing."

Dutifully, she scanned the living-room furniture and the shelves near the door where she stored some of her finished pottery. The TV was still there. And the computer. Nothing seemed out of place.

Burke followed her down the hall to her bedroom where she checked the contents of her jewelry box that rested on the knotty pine dresser. "Nothing appears to be missing, but the door to my walk-in closet is open. I didn't leave it that way."

"It might have been opened when we searched," he said. "Take a look inside."

Against the back wall was a neat row of dressy clothing, still in plastic dry cleaner's bags. Matching shoes were stored in their original boxes. She never wore those clothes anymore. They were part of her old life.

Jesse joined them. Though still pale, he seemed to have regained some of his strength. "I'll take over in here," he said to Burke. "You might want to keep an eye on the search."

"Thanks. Except for your man Wentworth, these guys aren't trained in forensics. They wouldn't know a clue if it jumped up and bit them on the ass." He gave Fiona a wave. "I'll be back."

Jesse came toward her. In spite of his slight limp and the black sling on his left arm, he moved with confidence.

"You seem better," she said.

"I'm getting a handle on these pain pills. Just a little foggy around the edges." He peeked around her into the closet. "Tidy."

"I haven't touched most of those things since I unpacked." She looked up into his eyes. His pupils were so dilated from the medication that she could barely see the dark cognac brown of his irises. "Maybe you should rest."

"When I need a nap, I'll let you know." He flashed that killer grin. "In the meantime, I'm your protector."

In spite of his light tone, she took him seriously. Her instincts told her this was a man she could trust with her life. In a way, she already had. Within moments of meeting Jesse, she'd told him the secret behind her move to the mountains. None of her friends in Denver knew how much she'd lost. Fiona's story was that she and Abby were going to live at the cabin and seek a more peaceful life. Peaceful? Not today!

She cleared her throat and said, "Burke told

me to look for signs that someone had been in my house."

"Keep at it."

She closed her closet door and led him into Abby's room, which was more cluttered than the rest of the house but didn't seem to have been ransacked.

"I can't imagine why anybody would want to rob me," she said. "I don't keep valuables here."

"From what you told me, you don't keep valuables at all."

"Things aren't important to me. I care about people. People matter."

He mattered. She'd only just met Jesse, but he mattered to her. Why was she so drawn to him? Very likely, because he was an incredibly good-looking man. His straight black hair was combed back from his forehead. He had high cheekbones, deep-set eyes and a firm jaw. But his features weren't perfect. His nose looked as if it had been broken more than once. And he had a scar on his chin. An interesting face.

"Let's go to the next room," he said.

The guest room with the colorful handmade quilt was neat as a pin. Again, the closet door stood open. It was the same in the den.

The only rooms left to search were the kitchen and her studio. She backtracked through the living room, passing the dining table where she and Abby had begun their Christmas decorating with a centerpiece of handmade clay elves and reindeer.

In the kitchen, her gaze went to the top of the fridge where she'd left the antique Colt .45. The rectangular box appeared to be unmoved. She should take it down and make sure the gun was still inside. But something else caught her attention.

"The apples." She pointed to a bowl on the table. "There are only three, and I'm sure I had four. I remember because I was going to run in here and grab an apple for Elvis."

"Elvis?"

"Carolyn's horse. She dropped by earlier." It seemed crazy that someone would break into her house for a healthy snack. "I could be wrong. Nothing else is out of place."

That left only her pottery studio. She went through the laundry room attached to the kitchen and stopped outside a closed door. "I always keep this door locked so Abby can't come in here unsupervised. Too many sharp implements. And a kiln."

She reached up for the key that hung from a hook near the top of the door frame. It was gone. Had she misplaced it?

Jesse reached past her and turned the doorknob. "It's open."

She stepped inside. Her potter's wheel was in one corner. The kiln in the other. The long table between them was cluttered with sketchbooks and current projects. On the opposite side of the room, tall storage cabinets against the wall were opened. The larger boxes had been dragged out to the center of the room and opened. "Someone was in here."

"Don't touch. There might be fingerprints." Using one of the sketching pencils, he opened the lid on one of the boxes and peered inside at an assortment of small kitchen appliances that she didn't use anymore. "Anything missing?"

"Hard to tell. That's just clutter."

"Your intruder didn't come here to rob you. He didn't take the flat-screen TV or the computer. I'd say he was looking for something specific."

But her house hadn't been torn apart. The drawers and cabinets in the kitchen were untouched. "He was searching for something big enough to fit into one of these boxes."

"Something that's about the size of a suitcase." With the fingers of his right hand, he raked his black hair off his forehead. "Something that's gone missing."

Fiona realized that she should have been frightened. The unlocked door and the boxes were evidence. *An intruder had been inside her house.* Instead, she felt angry and confused as she imagined a stranger wandering through her house, poking into her things. "I'm not in the mood for guessing games. What was he looking for?"

"The ransom," he said. "A million dollars in cash. That much money in small bills would fill a suitcase."

"Why would anyone think the ransom was in my house?"

"That's a million-dollar question."

"How about an answer?"

"Your property is close to the Carlisle's. If the kidnappers were on the run and had to stash the money, they might have stopped here."

"If so, they wouldn't have to search," she said. "They'd remember where they stashed it."

"There are two of them." He rested one hip on a high stool beside her worktable. "One of them might have decided he didn't want to share with his buddy. So he hid the money in your house. Now his buddy is looking for it."

She remembered the voices she'd heard last night. It has been late, after two o'clock. She couldn't make out the words but they sounded angry.

Her awareness of fear became reality. The danger—real danger—had come too close.

She stared through the window of her studio and saw the searchers approaching the barn. If anything was hidden here, they'd surely find it. But if they didn't, what should she do?

"Fiona." He spoke her name softly. "It's all right. Nothing bad is going to happen."

"How can you say that? Those men could have

come into my house last night. How would I have protected Abby?"

"I'm here now. I'll keep you and your daughter safe."

Panic shivered through her. She wanted to run, to get as far away from here as possible. But where could she go? She didn't have a house in Denver anymore, didn't have enough money to stay in a hotel. "I can't afford to hire you, Jesse."

"You already did. Remember? Pro bono."

She wasn't too proud to accept charity, especially when her daughter's safety was involved. Still, she asked, "Why?"

"I owe you," he said simply. "Your husband took a chance on hiring Longbridge Security when I was first starting out. Because I proved myself capable of protecting Wyatt Grant—the district attorney of Denver—my reputation was established. I've been busy ever since."

His calm tone and steady gaze bolstered her

confidence. Her fear began to recede. "You'll stay with me and Abby until this is over?"

"Your guest room looks comfortable."

Gratitude urged her toward him. Avoiding his sling, she hugged the right side of his body. "Thank you."

His right arm encircled her. For a long moment, they held each other in a clumsy embrace. Fiona had touched plenty of other men since her husband's death; she was an unrepentant hugger. But being this close to Jesse was different. His nearness awakened long-suppressed feelings of sensual warmth, the memory of what it was like to be a woman.

She stepped away from him. "There's something I need to give you."

She saw a subtle change in the way he looked at her. Had he felt it, too? The tiny sparks of passion that might ignite into a wildfire?

"You don't need to give me anything, Fiona."

"It's a bequest. Something Wyatt wanted you to have."

She turned on her heel and went back to the kitchen. Reaching up, she removed the polished oak box from the top of the refrigerator. It didn't seem right to just plop the box into his hands. This occasion required some kind of ceremony. "Are you well enough to walk?"

"Not for a twenty-mile trek," he said. "But I'm mobile."

"I'd like to take you to the place where I scattered Wyatt's ashes. That way I'll feel like he's with us."

Jesse nodded. "Lead on."

She took him out the front door and followed a single-file path that led through the white trunks of aspens surrounding the south side of the house. Over her shoulder, she said, "This property has been in Wyatt's family for generations. His great-grandfather built the cabin."

"But they weren't ranchers."

"Definitely not. The Grants were always professionals. Lawyers and doctors. They used the
cabin as a hunting lodge, a vacation place where
they could get away and relax."

Wyatt had loved coming up here. Every time
they made this trip from Denver, he told her it
felt as if he'd shoved his daily hassles and responsibilities in a bottom drawer and locked it
tight. At the cabin, he was free.

When he died, she knew this was where he
would want to be laid to rest—eternally a part
of the mountain landscape that fed his soul.

She turned to watch Jesse making his way along
the path. There was a slight hitch in his stride, not
even a full-fledged limp. His strength was returning, but she didn't want to push him too far.

At the edge of the aspen grove, she stood on
a rise overlooking a knee-high fence that surrounded a small plot of land. Four weathered
wooden crosses marked the graves of past generations. The hand-carved cross she'd made for

Wyatt still looked new. "In the summer," she said, "I plant flowers here. It's a nice view, don't you think?"

"Beautiful."

"Wyatt never forgot what you did for him, Jesse. In his will, he specifically requested that this gun be given to you."

She opened the case. Afternoon sunlight glistened on the silver barrel of the pearl-handled, antique Colt .45.

Jesse lifted the gun from the case, balancing it easily in his right hand. "I'll treasure this gift as much as I appreciate the memory of the good man who wanted me to have it."

A gust of wind kicked up, and she imagined Wyatt's spirit watching over them, approving of this moment between her and Jesse Longbridge.

He made his way closer to the small graveyard, circling a boulder that stood in the path. Abruptly, he came to a halt. His body tensed.

"What is it?" she asked.

He returned to her and placed the gun back in the case. "Go back to the house, Fiona. Get Burke and tell him to meet me here."

Though she trusted Jesse's judgment, she wouldn't allow herself to be brushed aside like a child. "You saw something."

"Let me save you from this nightmare." He positioned his body to block her view and held her arm, keeping her from going any farther on the path.

"I need to know."

"There is a dead man on the other side of this boulder. He's been murdered, and the coyotes have gotten to him."

She froze. Her blood ran cold. A dead, mutilated body. Here. Only a few steps away from her front door.

Chapter Five

Jesse clearly remembered the interior of the Carlisle ranch house from when he'd been here before. Generous-size rooms. Rustic but not old-fashioned. He sank into a chair on the far side of the dining-room table, mindful of the need to protect his injured shoulder from being accidentally bumped. Under the dressings that covered his wound, his skin felt damp, and he hoped it was only sweat, not blood oozing from the stitches. The pain had subsided to a dull throb. Though tempted to take another painkiller, he kept the amber vial in his pocket. He needed to be alert.

His job as a bodyguard was mainly reactive. He saw a threat and took action to stop it. His preparation consisted of briefings on possible enemies and memorizing dozens of photographs so he could scan a crowd and pick out those individuals who might pose a risk. His powers of observation were pretty good; he could tell the difference between a man reaching for a gun and a casual gesture.

When it came to his work, he was confident. In any situation—from a black-tie diplomatic reception to a ski slope in Aspen—he could assess the possible points of attack and take steps to avoid them. He and the men who worked for him at his Denver headquarters were expert marksmen, capable with a handgun or a sniper rifle. They were skilled drivers, knew hand-to-hand combat maneuvers and crowd control techniques.

But Jesse wasn't a detective. He left the crime solving to others…until now. This situation would tax a different section of his brain.

Burke had brought him to the Carlisle ranch house to look at mug shots. Hopefully, Jesse could identify the men who had shot him and grabbed Nicole. As for the dead man on Fiona's property, he couldn't tell if he'd seen that person before. Half of his face had been gnawed off by indigenous scavengers, like coyotes and mountain lions.

Fiona fidgeted behind the chair at the head of the table, too agitated to sit. She'd asked to come along, preferring not to be at her house while it was being processed by the Delta County Sheriff's Department. Her voice was low and worried. "What if Abby had found the body? What if she'd run down the hill, playing a game with her imaginary pony, and stumbled over a dead man?"

"It didn't happen that way," he said.

"You're right. No need to borrow trouble when I've got plenty of my own problems." She rested her palms on the tabletop leaned toward him, staring intently. "How are you doing?"

What the hell was she up to? "Is there a reason you're right up in my face?"

"I'm checking your eyeballs for dilation."

"Don't." He wasn't her patient. "I'm fine."

Looking down, he glided his fingers on the surface of the table. Someone had recently dusted and cleaned. Underlying the lemony scent of furniture polish was another fragrance. *Coffee!* Though he hadn't eaten solid food in three days, he wasn't really hungry. But he deeply craved a rich dose of caffeine.

A tall, slim woman with black hair charged into the room. She held out her hand to him. "I'm Carolyn Carlisle."

"I know." He shook her hand, remembering that she was the first person who had gotten to him after he was shot. "You tried to stop my bleeding. Thank you."

"You're the one who deserves thanks," she said. "You risked your life to help my family. You're a hero, Jesse. If there's anything I can do for you, just ask."

"A cup of coffee," he said. "Black."

"I'll get it," Fiona said. She darted toward the kitchen.

Burke strode into the dining room and placed a laptop computer on the table. Though he only briefly glanced toward Carolyn, Jesse recognized the look of love in his eyes.

"Just a few hours ago," Burke said, "this dining room was command central for the kidnapping. There were banks of computers and dozens of agents."

"Why was the search called off?" Jesse asked.

"We had accomplished our secondary objective," Agent Burke explained. "The survivalist group, known as the Sons of Freedom or SOF, rented the Circle M. Computer forensics showed they were linked to a smuggling operation. Guns and drugs. Additionally, their leader is suspected of murder. We've arrested the perpetrators, and relocated the witnesses into protective custody."

"What about the primary objective? The kidnapping."

"My brother wanted the FBI gone," Carolyn said. "After Dylan talked to Nicole, he was convinced that she's all right and doesn't want to come home."

No victim meant no crime. Jesse understood that part of the equation, but a million dollars had gone missing. "What about the ransom? That money is as much Carolyn's as Dylan's."

"True," she said through gritted teeth. "And I want the ransom back. But Dylan called off the investigation. He's saying that the million dollars is a divorce settlement."

"Assuming that it went to Nicole," Jesse said. "That she ran off with one of her abductors."

"Finding the body at Fiona's house sheds a new light on the situation," Burke said. "We'll have to wait for DNA to be certain of his identity. Based on his height, hair color and the custom-made belt buckle, I'm pretty sure the dead man is Butch Thurgood."

Jesse had never heard the name before. "Was he one of the kidnappers?"

"You tell me." Burke placed the computer in front of him. "Scroll down and tell me if you recognize the men who shot you."

Concentrating, Jesse stared at the computer screen. Though he didn't have a clear view of Nicole's abductors, he'd been close enough, and he was good at remembering faces. The line of a jaw. The curve of a nose.

The first three images were unfamiliar. Then came the fourth. "This man," he said. "He's the one who shot me."

"Are you sure?"

Jesse studied the weak chin and narrow lines of the face. In the computer image, his eyes were visible. His cruelty, apparent. "He didn't have as much facial hair as in this photo, but this is him."

"Pete Richter," Carolyn said.

Tapping the computer key, Jesse looked at other faces. Most of them were average—the kind of men who didn't stand out in a crowd. One of them looked like a cowboy from the Old West with a thick mustache and lantern jaw. "This might be the victim we found at Fiona's place."

"Is he the other kidnapper?"

Jesse shook his head. "The guy who grabbed Nicole was fair-haired. No mustache."

He stopped on another image. "This is the second kidnapper. He's the one who said that Dylan would pay a lot of money to get his wife back."

Carolyn gasped. "It's Sam Logan. Damn him. I should have known."

"Logan was the leader of the SOF," Burke explained. "We suspected he was behind the kidnapping but didn't think he was also the primary kidnapper."

"He's been taken into custody?"

"Correct."

Jesse had a lot more questions about the delivery of the ransom and the evidence that had been gathered in the prior investigation. "I'd like to review your files on the case."

"It's all on this laptop," Burke said.

"If you print it out, I can take a copy with me. I'll be staying at Fiona's until we're sure there's no danger to her or her daughter."

"Good plan," Carolyn said with obvious relief. "I was going to suggest that she and Abby move over here, but I'm sure the little girl would feel better in her own house."

Fiona marched back into the dining room

with a tray that she placed in front of Jesse. "Milk and oatmeal," she said.

"No coffee?"

"Not until you have something else in your stomach. You probably haven't eaten solid food for days."

He glared into the bowl of mushy oatmeal. "I want coffee."

"After you're finished with this," she said.

Being treated like an invalid wasn't his thing. Even though he'd been injured. Even though he'd technically died for a couple of minutes.

But Fiona stood firm. She was so determined to nurture him that she just might pick up the spoon and start feeding him herself.

Reluctantly, he shoveled in a mouthful of oatmeal. Sweetened with brown sugar, it didn't taste half bad. But it was heavy, thick. When he forced himself to swallow, it felt as if he could trace the lump through his digestive system.

He looked up at Burke. "How about it? Can I look at your files?"

"This is official FBI business. Technically, I shouldn't share." He looked toward Carolyn. "But I've already broken too many rules to count, and I'd like your input."

"I appreciate your trust." Jesse washed down another bite of oatmeal with a swig of milk.

Fiona turned to Burke and asked, "When do you think the sheriff will be done with my house? I need to pick up my daughter from the babysitter."

"A couple more hours," Burke said. "They're looking for prints and other forensic evidence. And they have to process the body."

"Have dinner with us," Carolyn said. "I know Abby loves to be around the horses."

"Wonderful." Fiona beamed. "Maybe we can get started with those Christmas decorations."

While the two women chatted about Christmas trees and family ornaments, Jesse worked on his food. His gut roiled, but he knew Fiona was right. He needed solid food. He needed to recover his full strength.

When he looked up from the nearly empty bowl, he saw Dylan Carlisle standing in the dining-room entryway. A few days ago, when he'd first met Dylan, Jesse had the impression that he was dealing with a strong, reliable man who was capable of running a cattle ranching empire. The tall, lean cowboy who stood so silently was a pale reflection of his former self.

Dylan's shoulders were stooped. His clothes, rumpled. The circles around his green eyes made him look as though he'd been punched in the face. His cheeks were hollow. Losing his wife had nearly destroyed him.

"I'm glad to see you've recovered, Jesse." Dylan's voice was as cold as a January blizzard. "As of now, your services are no longer required."

Apparently, Dylan didn't share Carolyn's opinion about Jesse being a hero. As he rose from the table to face the devastated man, Jesse felt the bitter ache of failure. There was truth in Dylan's accusation. He'd been hired to protect the Carlisle family, and he had failed.

"I want to see this through," Jesse said.

"There's nothing more to do."

"Don't be ridiculous," Carolyn snapped at her brother. "We still need security. They just found a dead body at Fiona's place."

Dylan looked at Fiona as if seeing her for the first time. "Is Abby okay?"

"She wasn't home, thank God."

"It was one of the kidnappers," Carolyn said. "Butch Thurgood."

Dylan's eyes narrowed. "Thurgood? The horse whisperer?"

"We need to keep investigating," she said. "That's why Burke is here, and I want to keep Longbridge Security."

"Damn it, Carolyn. It's over. Can't you get it through your head? Nicole isn't coming back. She doesn't want to be with me anymore."

"I want to offer my services," Jesse said. "No charge."

"Haven't you done enough?" Dylan lurched forward and braced his hands on the table. "You were supposed to keep us safe."

"That's not fair," Carolyn protested. "Nicole didn't follow protocol. She went riding off by herself without telling Jesse."

"She's never coming back to me." Dylan straightened. "She's gone."

"Listen to me." Fiona's gentle voice cut through the tension. "Dylan, you might be giving up on Nicole too soon."

When he turned to look at her, pain twisted his features. "She turned her back. She walked away."

"I've lost someone I loved," Fiona said. "I understand your sorrow. But I'll tell you this.

If I could have one more minute with my husband, I'd go through hell to get it."

"What if he didn't want you?"

With her long brown braid and her quiet manner, Fiona seemed delicate—so fragile that a gust of wind could blow her away. But she had an unshakeable inner strength. "I'd still fight for him."

Her words resonated. The relationship she'd had with her husband was deep and true. Special. Jesse hoped that, someday, he could find a connection like that—a love that went beyond the grave.

Dylan turned away. "I want no part of this."

He left the room quickly.

From down the hallway, Jesse heard a door slam. He turned to Carolyn. "I'm leaving two men here at the house. Wentworth and Neville. I'll be staying at Fiona's."

"You're welcome to stay for dinner," she said.

"It's better for me to leave."

He didn't want to face Dylan again. Not until he had something to report.

PETE RICHTER LIKED being up high, above it all. In the nest he'd made in a pine tree, twenty feet off the ground, he was damn near invisible. Not many people looked up when they were searching. They were too stupid. They kept their eyes on the dirt.

He looked down at the Carlisle ranch house, peering through small binoculars for a better view. He was close enough to hear them talking but couldn't make out the words.

All the feds, except that one guy who was having sex with the high and mighty Carolyn Carlisle, had left early this morning, taking their chopper and sniffer dogs along with them. They'd arrested Logan and everybody else in the SOF. Fine with him. As far as he was concerned, they could all go to hell.

He leaned back against the rough pine bark.

Years ago, when he worked as a lumberjack in Oregon, he had stayed in the treetops all day. Except for the cold, he was comfortable. Earlier, he'd used a hand ax—a tool he carried on his belt—to chop away the small branches that poked into his back. This was a good perch for a watcher, even better for a sniper. If he'd wanted, he could have taken aim from here and picked off ten men before they noticed him.

But that wasn't his plan.

As soon as he found his share of the ransom, his five-hundred-thousand-dollar share, he intended to leave the West to the cowboys and their stinking cattle. He'd move to Baja. Live on the beach. Climb the palm trees and get coconuts for food. He'd never work again.

If damn Butch Thurgood hadn't double-crossed him, he could have been in Mexico right now. He should have known better than to trust Butch. That cowboy had been coasting on his rodeo reputation for years, but he was weak.

Richter hadn't meant to kill him. When he started hitting Butch, he only wanted to punish him, to make him talk. But things got out of hand. Butch made him mad. Real mad.

He remembered using his gloved fist, punching again and again. Then he'd picked up a rock. Butch died with his eyes wide open, staring up in surprise.

Hearing voices from the ranch house, Richter peered down. He saw the security guard he'd shot leaving the house with the fed. They got into a truck and drove south, toward the widow Grant's property where the sheriff and his deputies were digging around and searching.

The worst thing that could happen was for one of those lamebrain deputies to find the ransom. But they weren't that smart. He'd already gone through the outbuildings on the widow's land. And he hadn't found a damn thing.

Still, he knew the money was there. Butch didn't have time to move it. But where? The way

Richter figured, the widow had to know. Maybe she'd been working with Butch. Or maybe she found the money and stashed it herself.

Either way, Pete needed to get his hands on Fiona Grant. He'd make her talk.

Chapter Six

Sunset painted the December skies in streaks of pink and gold above distant, snowy peaks. For a moment, Jesse watched and marveled. He'd almost died. This might count as the first sunset of the rest of his life. Inborn wisdom told him to take a moment to appreciate this miracle of light.

He sat on the one-step covered porch outside Fiona's front door. Beside him was Sheriff Trainer from Delta. His deputies had removed the body and dusted for prints. They were still combing the area—looking for evidence and finding nothing of importance.

The sheriff took a drag on his cigarette. "I've been around a long time. Never been tangled up in anything this complicated, but I've dealt with my share of lawbreakers. And it seems to me that when people get in trouble, they're usually asking for it."

"Not in my line of work," Jesse said. "Most of the people I'm hired to protect are victims of circumstance. Like the Carlisles. Like Nicole."

"Miss Nicole was in the wrong place at the wrong time," the sheriff conceded. "Those boys from the SOF didn't set out to kidnap anybody. But you've got to admit that they wouldn't have kept Nicole if she hadn't been Dylan's wife. They knew he'd pay any price to get her back."

"Are you saying that it's Nicole's fault that she got kidnapped?"

"Hell, no. I'm not blaming her." His long, narrow face grew even longer when he frowned. "I might be a rural county sheriff, but I'm not an idiot."

"Didn't say you were."

But he'd thought it. Before the kidnapping and murder, Sheriff Trainer might have been a good-natured, easy-going guy. Now he was as nervous as a squirrel guarding his winter cache of pinecones.

"I'm trying to make a point," Trainer said. "There's got to be a reason why the kidnappers are searching here."

Jesse knew where the sheriff's logic was headed. They'd all been asking the same question: why here? Logic pointed toward Fiona. She must have done something to bring trouble upon herself.

He also knew that those assumptions were dead wrong. His instincts told him that Fiona was completely, entirely innocent.

The sheriff looked down at the growing ash on his cigarette and asked, "How well do you know Fiona Grant?"

"I met her for the first time today," he said. "But I knew her husband. A good man who died too young."

The sheriff shot a glance toward Jesse. "Do you think she's got something to hide?"

"Hell, no."

Not Fiona. Not that sweet, gentle woman with the appealing gray eyes. When they found the opened boxes in her pottery studio, she was genuinely surprised. Until he mentioned the ransom, the thought hadn't occurred to her. When they discovered the body of Butch Thurgood, he'd seen her terror.

"It doesn't make sense, Sheriff. If she knew where the ransom was stashed, why wouldn't she grab it and run?"

"Could be that Butch hid the ransom before she got her hands on it."

"Think again," Jesse said. "If she knew the ransom was here, she'd want to keep it a secret. She wouldn't call in a search party."

"Unless she was scared. Pete Richter is still at large," the sheriff reminded him. "Maybe she decided it was better to hand over the cash than to face Richter's vengeance."

Though he had a counterargument for everything Jesse said, it was all speculation. "You seem to be drawing a hell of a lot of assumptions based on zero evidence."

He stubbed out his cigarette. "If the ransom is hidden here, it seems like Fiona would know something about it."

"You're wasting your time suspecting her," Jesse said. "In my line of work, I need to read people. And I'm good at my job. I can look at a crowd and know from their faces and body language if they're dangerous. Believe me when I tell you this—Fiona Grant isn't a liar or a criminal."

"You have to say that." The sheriff rose slowly and stretched. "She hired you as a bodyguard. You're her employee, and I'll bet she's paying you a pretty penny. She must have inherited a ton of money when her husband died."

"If that's true…" Which it wasn't, but Jesse didn't have the right to tell the sheriff or anyone else about her distressed financial situation. "Why would she be interested in the ransom money?"

"Don't know. But I'm making it my business to find out."

Jesse stood as Wentworth came out on the porch and announced, "I've done the best I can to make sure the house is secure for the night. Windows are all locked. I installed braces on the front and back doors."

"Good work," Jesse said.

"I'd feel a lot better about Fiona's safety if we called down to the Denver office and got Max up here to install a real security system."

Max Milton was one of Jesse's most valued employees. He couldn't shoot, wasn't in top physical condition, and wore glasses an inch thick. But his ability with computers and electronics was first-rate.

Jesse had already checked in with his office manager, who told him the other five bodyguards who worked for him were all on the job, as was Max, who was on-site in Cheyenne, Wyoming, setting up security at an auto parts warehouse. "I arranged for Max to come here when he's finished with his current project."

"How's everything in the office?"

Jesse knew that Wentworth really wanted to know about their office manager, who happened to be his sister. "Elena is just fine. She likes being in charge. And she's better at coordinating things than I am."

With a sheepish grin, Wentworth said, "Someday, we're all going to be working for Elena."

"Don't tell her that. She already thinks she's the boss."

The sheriff took another cigarette out of his pack. "I think we're done here. My boys are just about packed up and ready to leave."

Good riddance as far as Jesse was concerned. The sheriff's suspicions regarding Fiona were way off base. Why the hell was he so anxious to put the blame on her? Because he had secrets of his own?

His chain-smoking and nervousness could be signs of a guilty conscience. Perhaps Sheriff Trainer had something to hide.

WHILE THEY HAD BEEN EATING dinner at the Carlisle Ranch, Fiona tried to find a way to explain to Abby that bad things had been happening. But how could she tell a four-year-old about a dead man on their doorstep? How could she explain that Nicole had been kidnapped? In an ideal world, children didn't need to know about such things.

As she drove home with Abby buckled into her car seat in the back of the station wagon, Fiona tried again. "Do you remember in pre-school when Officer Crowley came to talk to your class?"

"Stranger danger," Abby said. "Don't talk to people you don't know. Don't take candy. Run away fast."

"You need to remember those lessons. Even at our house."

"Okay."

"We have someone who will help us. A man who's going to stay with us for a few days. His name is Jesse Longbridge."

"Does he have a horse?"

"I don't think so." But he did own a gun. Should she talk to Abby about gun safety? "He was a friend of your daddy."

"Then he's my friend, too."

A child's view of life was so wonderfully simple. "If you have any questions about anything, talk to me about it. Okay?"

"Okay, Mommy."

Their short ride was over. Fiona parked outside the garage, not wanting to pull inside where it was dark. She'd always been afraid of shadows, and now she had a tangible reason to avoid the dark corners.

After she unbuckled Abby from her car seat, she held her daughter's hand and walked toward the front door. Sheriff Trainer had been considerate enough not to festoon her house in yellow crime scene tape. Though some of the low-lying shrubs had been trampled, her log cabin looked pretty much the same. The curtains were drawn, but the porch lamp glowed cheerfully.

Jesse opened the front door before they got there. The porch light shone on his thick black hair. Standing above them on the porch, he appeared taller than his six-foot height. Though he was lean, his shoulders were wide. He looked strong and capable, even with his left arm in a sling. She was incredibly glad that he was staying with them.

He ushered them inside quickly and closed the door. When she introduced him to Abby, he squatted down to the child's level and extended his good hand. "Pleased to meet you," he said.

Abby's blue eyes brightened as she shook his large hand and studied him. With her blond curls and dimples, she looked like a little pixie. "Jesse, are you an Indian?"

"Navajo," he said. "Half Navajo."

"Navajo," she repeated. "Thank you for the maize and turkey you gave the pilgrims."

Fiona wasn't surprised that Abby remembered the Thanksgiving stories she'd learned in pre-school. This year, when she and her daughter were celebrating, Abby insisted on doing her own version of the Thanksgiving story, complete with dancing turkeys and a singing yam.

"That wasn't my tribe," Jesse said. "But you're welcome."

"How come you don't wear a feather?"

Though Fiona winced at the stereotyping, Jesse grinned. "Different tribes wear different clothes, but we all believe in hospitality and sharing. I have a gift for you."

"You do?"

Jesse stood and went to the hooks by the front door where his denim jacket with the Longbridge Security patch was hanging. From an inner pocket, he took out a small leather bag and opened the drawstring. "My grandfather was a wise man, and he gave me many totems."

"What's a totem?" Abby asked.

"It can protect you. Or it can remind you of your heritage or your dreams. A totem can be anything. A necklace or a coin or a picture."

"I have a locket with a note inside from my daddy. It says, 'I love you, Abigail.'"

Fiona's heart clenched. Though she tried to shield her daughter, life happened. Her father was dead, and Abby understood the importance of cherishing the past while looking toward the future. Quite possibly, she'd learned that lesson better than her mother.

Though the limited use of his left hand made him slightly clumsy, Jesse opened the bag and took out a small blue stone. In an open palm, he held it toward Abby. "It's turquoise. This stone will bring you luck."

"Thank you." Solemnly, she took it from him. "When I get my pony, I'm going to name him Turquoise."

"That's a wonderful idea," Fiona said, "and we'll talk about it tomorrow."

"My pony will have a blue tail."

"I'm sure he will." She smiled. "Now, it's late. You need to get ready for bed. Don't forget to—"

"Brush my teeth." Abby twirled once and scampered off toward her room.

Jesse rose stiffly and stretched his shoulders. "She's bright."

Of course, Fiona agreed. "Smart, pretty and healthy. Everything a child should be."

"You've been a good mother."

She wasn't so sure about that part of the equation. After Wyatt died, she'd been depressed and not as responsive to Abby as she should have been. And she hadn't handled the disbursement of her husband's inheritance well. Thank goodness, she'd hung on to Abby's trust fund. When her daughter turned eighteen, there would be sufficient money for her to go to college and get a decent start on her life.

But that was a long time away, and Fiona had more immediate concerns. She looked toward Jesse. "Did the sheriff figure out who was snooping around my house?"

"No proof, but plenty of fingerprints," he said. "Let me show you the security we've installed."

At the front door, he showed her how to use a brace that held the door shut even if the lock was unlatched. Additional dead bolts had been added on front and back doors. She was familiar with security systems. "Our home in Denver had an electronic burglar alarm with a keypad."

"Wyatt knew how to take precautions. I'm kind of surprised that he didn't have more up here. From what you've told me, this house is vacant for weeks at a time."

"Months," she said. "We hardly ever came up here in winter. Wyatt used to pay a caretaker. After he died, I hired someone to stay here full-time."

"A local?"

"The same woman who babysits Abby," she said. "She has a little boy who's the same age as Abby, and sometimes I take care of him. When she separated from her husband, having her stay at my house was a good solution for both of us. She had a place to live. And I had somebody who could handle the upkeep. Her name is Belinda Miller."

"Sounds familiar."

"She's Nate Miller's ex-wife." She frowned. Though Belinda always swore that Nate hadn't abused her, he was that type—mean-spirited and angry at the world. "He owns the Circle M Ranch. But he wasn't part of the survivalist group. He was only leasing his property to them."

"Nate Miller." Jesse repeated the name. She had the sense that he was storing that bit of information away in the back of his head. She knew he'd been reading Burke's case files while she and Abby were at dinner. Jesse probably had a great deal of information on the locals.

He asked, "Was Belinda living here when you decided to move back?"

"A few months ago, she moved in with her boyfriend in Riverton. He's a decent man. Works at the meatpacking plant in Delta."

"Did Belinda continue her duties as caretaker?"

"Absolutely. She came up here two or three times a week to make sure everything was okay."

"Did she know people from the survivalist group?"

Fiona was taken aback. If he was hinting that Belinda might have something to do with the missing ransom, he could forget it. "She's my friend. A good friend. Abby and Mickey are nearly inseparable."

"I'm glad Abby has someone to play with."

Living here at the cabin with no nearby neighbors was far too isolated for her gregarious daughter. Abby needed to be around other kids. "After the first of the year, Belinda and I are hoping to organize a cooperative preschool for the local toddlers. Maybe a kindergarten, too. The regular grade school is all the way in Delta. That's a forty-minute ride on a school bus for Abby."

"Like I said, Fiona, you're a good mom."

His gaze came to rest upon her, and she suddenly felt self-conscious. Messy strands of hair had escaped her long braid. She hadn't bothered with makeup this morning, and her clothes felt clammy against her skin. It would have been nice to present herself in a better light to Jesse. She wanted him to appreciate her, maybe even to think she was attractive.

She hadn't dated since Wyatt's death, hadn't cared what anybody thought of her appearance. *Now I care. I definitely care.*

Warmth flooded her cheeks. She stood a little straighter, aware that the waistband on her jeans was too loose. She'd lost too much weight. All her shirts drooped straight down from her shoulders. *I want to be pretty again.*

Turning away from him, she peeled off her green corduroy jacket and draped it on a peg by the door. "Have you eaten?"

"No more oatmeal," he said. "How are you at solving puzzles?"

"I can usually make things fit together." Her fingers laced together. "Working with clay gives me a good sense of space and balance."

"This isn't about spatial relationships. It's logic."

She winced. "Not my best thing."

"I can use your help, anyway. I've been going over the crime files on the computer Burke gave me. There's a rational sequence of events, but I'm missing something."

She glanced down the hall toward her daughter's bedroom. "After Abby goes to sleep, we can go over the files."

Suddenly alert, he pivoted on his heel and strode toward the window. "Someone's coming."

"What?"

"Don't you hear the approaching vehicle?"

She listened hard, vaguely hearing the sound of a car engine. "I'm not expecting anyone."

Jesse moved to the edge of the window and peeked through the drapes. "A silver SUV. Cadillac."

She never paid attention to cars, but she knew one family who drove only Cadillacs. It couldn't be them! Fate wouldn't be so cruel. She had enough to worry about.

The car door slammed with a solid thunk. She came close to Jesse and looked through the window. When she saw the driver emerge, she gasped. He looked like her late husband—a younger version. He had Wyatt's walk. His blond hair was curly, like Wyatt's. For a moment, she thrilled to a deeply embedded memory—seeing Wyatt come home from work, come home to her waiting arms.

But this young man despised her.

"It's Wyatt's son from his first marriage. Clinton Grant."

Chapter Seven

Years ago, Fiona met her stepson for the first time at a Grant family dinner that took place a few weeks before her wedding.

Clinton had been a sullen teenager who resented her and blamed her for the failure of his parents' marriage even though Wyatt and his first wife were divorced for over a year before Fiona met him. The first words young Clinton had spoken to her were "You're too young for my father. And you aren't even pretty."

His mother had laughed at his unsubtle inference to Fiona as a trophy wife. Clinton's younger sister had merely glared.

Fiona's pride had ruled the day. She refused to be drawn into a bitching match. Without hurling a single insult, she lifted her chin and walked away.

That brief exchange set the tone for all future confrontations. Even now, when Clinton was all grown up, a graduate of law school who had already started work in the family firm, his attitude toward Fiona had not mellowed.

He hammered on the front door. With each heavy thud of his fist, her anger ratcheted higher, but she refused to let Clinton know how much he affected her. Over the years, she'd always faced him with ice, not fire.

She stiffened her spine and opened the door. "Clinton, I'm so surprised to see you. Unfortunately, this isn't a convenient time."

He peered past her shoulder and saw Jesse. "Am I interrupting a booty call?"

"May I introduce Jesse Longbridge? He's my bodyguard."

"Whatever." He stepped forward, but she didn't move. "Let me in, Fiona."

"Not convenient," she repeated.

"I'd advise you to step aside. Otherwise, I'll be back with the sheriff and a warrant. You have several items that belong to me."

Clinton and his mother had already taken more than their fair share. After Wyatt's death, they swooped in like vultures. Now he was back to pick the bones. "I have no idea what you're talking about."

"Heirlooms," he said. "Valuable objects that have been in my family for generations."

Before she could slam the door in his face, Abby flew into the room and wedged her way in front of her mother. Wearing her pink flannel pajamas, she beamed at Clinton and held up her little hand. "High five."

Not even a greedy creep like Clinton could

resist Abby's charm. His mouth loosened in a grin as he slapped hands with her. "High five."

She tugged on his trouser leg, pulling him into the house. "I'm going to get a pony," she said. "And his name is going to be Turquoise, and he'll have a long, curly blue tail."

Clenching her jaw to keep from screaming, Fiona stepped aside. Abby was at that curious age when everything interested her: bugs, snakes and obnoxious stepbrothers.

Her daughter pushed Clinton to the dining-room table and ordered him to sit. When he was seated, she cocked her head to one side, then the other. Clinton played along, matching her movements. The physical resemblance between them was obvious. And somewhat depressing.

Playing hostess, Abby said, "Me and Mommy will bring you a healthy snack."

"No snacks," Fiona said. "It's past your bedtime."

"But, Mommy, it's polite."

Her daughter had picked a lousy time to remember proper behavior. Fiona couldn't bear the thought of sitting down at the table with Clinton.

Jesse stepped forward. "Let's go, Abby. I want you to show me your room. We'll leave your mom and Clinton alone for a while. They have something important to talk about."

"More important than a pony?"

He chuckled as he led her from the room. "I don't suppose there's anything more important than a blue-tail pony."

As soon as they left, Fiona confronted Clinton. Her icy veneer was beginning to melt under the heat of her anger. "Don't ever use my daughter to get to me. Leave Abby out of this."

"But my little stepsister loves me."

"Just tell me what you want."

He reached into the inner pocket of his Harris tweed sports coat and took out an inventory sheet, which he placed on the table so she could see it. "This is it."

Over twenty items were listed, ranging from a Tiffany lamp to a pink crystal tiara. Fiona pushed the list back toward him with one finger. "I don't have any of this stuff. Nor would I want it. Out here in cattle country, there isn't much call for tiaras."

"Then you shouldn't mind if I take a look around." A purely evil sneer distorted his handsome face. "Abby can help me search. We'll make it a treasure hunt."

The fact that he wanted to recruit her daughter to help in his scheme almost blinded her to the more obvious truth. "You want to search my property."

"If you were more cooperative—"

"Were you here before? Did you enter my house without my permission?"

"Of course not."

She didn't believe him. It wasn't a stretch to

imagine Clinton sneaking into her house and searching. He could have pulled out the large box in her studio while looking for a Tiffany lamp she never owned. This scenario made a hundred times more sense than kidnappers searching for a ransom.

"It was you," she said. "You saw me leave with Carolyn, and you took advantage of my absence to search."

"I don't know what you're talking about."

Grasping at shreds of her composure, she said, "Please leave."

"You're crazy, Fiona."

He was dangerously close to being right. She was mad, mad, mad. "Please. Leave us alone."

"Or else? What are you going to do? Sic your bodyguard on me?"

Right on cue, Jesse appeared behind him. "You heard the lady. It's time for you to go."

Clinton stood to confront him. In his tweed jacket and cashmere sweater, he resembled an old-fashioned gentleman, the lord of the manor. Fiona wouldn't be surprised if he took a formal pugilistic stance with his fists raised.

But he didn't dare.

Even with his arm in a sling, Jesse exuded masculine confidence. If it came to a physical fight, he could handle Clinton without breaking a sweat. Jesse's dark eyes shone with a hard, cold strength. He meant business.

And Clinton didn't challenge him. Her stepson might be pushy and underhanded, but he wasn't stupid.

He stalked toward the door, yanked it open and turned back toward her. "You need to pull yourself together, Fiona. This isn't a fit environment for raising a child. If you're not careful, you might lose Abby, too."

His threat went way over the top. There was no way in hell he could dispute her custody of Abby. The idea was not only absurd but infuriating. How dare he even suggest that she wasn't a fit mother! Her self-control shattered. She was beyond mad.

She thrust her hand toward Jesse. "Give me your gun."

Clinton gaped. "What are you doing?"

"Something I should have done a long time ago. Teaching you some manners."

"You can't—"

"I'm within my rights. Around here, we shoot trespassers."

He slammed the door as he left.

Rage swirled around her like a red tornado, but she was calm in the eye of the storm. *This is what it feels like to defend your home.*

It felt damned good.

JESSE WAITED AT THE dining-room table for Fiona to finish reading Abby a bedtime story. Her attack on Clinton had surprised him. Who knew she was such a firecracker?

He'd overheard enough of her earlier conversation with her stepson to know that she suspected him of breaking into her house and going through her things. In a way, he hoped her accusation was true. Clinton was a mean son of a bitch who took pleasure in harassing a widow, but he presented less of a threat than Pete Richter.

Unfortunately, Jesse didn't believe that Clinton was the culprit. Sure, he had a motive to search for his supposedly valuable things. But no reason to murder Butch Thurgood. Nor could Jesse imagine the polished young lawyer creeping around in the forest, waiting for his opportunity to sneak inside and search.

Fiona's stepson was another piece of a big puzzle where nothing fit together right. Too many details about the kidnapping and the kidnappers—from the haphazard way Nicole was abducted to her refusal to come home—were skewed.

The only part that made sense was the way

Burke and the FBI had closed down the survivalist smuggling operation. Using high-tech precision, they took all the men into custody and protected the women and children from harm. They'd even rescued a pregnant woman in the throes of childbirth who was still at the Delta hospital, accompanied by one of the FBI profilers, Mike Silverman, who seemed to have formed an attachment to the new mother and child. According to Burke's notes, Silverman was taking a leave of absence so he could escort the mother and child home to her parents.

Fiona came to the table and sank into the chair to his right. She folded her arms on the tabletop and rested her forehead upon them. While she'd been putting Abby to sleep, she'd unfastened her long braid. Her long brown hair tumbled around her shoulders in shiny waves.

He reached over and stroked her hair. His intention was to comfort her, but another urge rose up within him. He wanted to caress her, to pull her toward him and feel her slender body pressed against him. From the first moment he saw her, he'd been drawn to her quiet beauty. He liked her spirit, her warmth, even the anger that hinted at a deeper passion.

Only one thing held him back. He couldn't help thinking of her as another man's wife. She'd never stopped loving her husband.

She lifted her head and looked at him with tired gray eyes. "It's been a long day."

Reluctantly, he withdrew his hand from her shoulder. "Very long."

"You must be exhausted."

"Hell, no. I slept for three days in the hospital. I'm fine." Not exactly true. He'd been taking pain meds, and his body was sore. He was worried about how he'd stay awake tonight to keep watch. "Tell me something. If I'd given you my gun, would you have shot him?"

She grinned and pushed the curtain of hair away from her face. "I wanted to. But I don't think I could have pulled the trigger. It would probably upset Abby if I killed her stepbrother."

"Probably."

"By the way, thank you for giving her that turquoise stone. She loves it. And now you're on her Christmas list."

"I don't need a present."

"Making Christmas presents is as much fun for her as giving them. She's sculpting little clay figures that we fire in the kiln. A lot of them are ponies."

Her mention of Christmas reminded him of a possibility that would ensure her safety more effectively than having him here as a bodyguard. She could go home. "Do you have family nearby?"

"My parents are archeologists. A couple of months ago, they rented out their house in California and went to a dig site in Peru."

"You have no one you could stay with until the threat of danger passes?"

"There's Wyatt's family. They all adore Abby, and most of them aren't as obnoxious as Clinton. But I wouldn't be a welcome guest." She tossed her head. "I'd rather stay here. We're safe. Aren't we?"

He wished that he could reassure her, but he wouldn't soon forget the ravaged corpse in her front yard. "I can't guarantee it. Not while Richter is still at large."

A series of emotions played across her face. A frightened twitch. A worried frown. Her gaze flicked upward as if searching for an answer. She was one of the most open people he'd ever known, utterly without guile.

Her jaw set. She showed determination. "We'd better figure out this puzzle and get Richter arrested."

He turned the computer screen toward her. "You can read Burke's case file."

With a gesture that managed to convey exhaustion and disgust, she waved the laptop away. Her hands were nearly as expressive as her face. "I'm too tired to read. You can tell me the important points."

With a nod, he started at the beginning. "Nicole was kidnapped by Richter and Logan and taken to the Circle M. When Burke interviewed Logan, he learned that Logan—the leader of the SOF survivalists—sent Nicole away with Richter and Thurgood for safekeeping."

"He told Burke that?"

"Logan is in custody and talking his head off, hoping to make a deal. He says that after Richter and Thurgood took Nicole, he never saw her again."

"Does Burke believe him?"

"There's no evidence that shows Richter and Thurgood returned to the Circle M. But Nicole herself gave them the clue that she was there."

"How?"

"Proof of life," Jesse said. "Standard operating procedure in kidnap cases is to demand proof that the victim is still alive. Here's the first photo of Nicole."

On the computer screen, he pulled up a still picture of Nicole with a newspaper showing the day's headline. "Look at the way she's holding the paper. Her fingers form a circle and an M."

"She doesn't look scared at all." Fiona leaned closer to thc screen. "I wouldn't have been that brave."

"Sure you would. I saw how you stood up to Clinton."

"Dealing with a jerk isn't comparable to being held captive."

"Keep in mind," Jesse reminded her, "that Nicole might have been falling in love with one of the kidnappers, probably Butch Thurgood. He was a former rodeo star and an accomplished horseman."

"And she's a large-animal veterinarian. I guess they have a lot in common."

Because Fiona was so sensitive, he was interested in her interpretation of Nicole's actions. "Do you think she's the kind of woman who'd run off with a kidnapper?"

"It sounds kind of romantic. Some women are attracted to bad boys. But I thought Dylan and Nicole were truly, deeply in love." She shook her head. "I could be wrong. It's hard to know what goes on inside a marriage."

Jesse tapped a few computer keys and played a video. Nicole looked into the camera and said she'd be fine if they paid the ransom. "Again, watch her hands. She made a circle when she tucked her hair behind her ears. The way she touched her lips is a sideways M."

"The way she's dressed," Fiona said. "It isn't right. She wears practical ranching clothes. Not a worn-out cotton shirt with a flower print."

In Burke's notes, others had come to the same conclusion. "Here's the third proof of life. Another video."

He and Fiona watched and listened as Nicole apologized for causing so much trouble and said everything might have worked out for the best.

"No clue this time," Fiona said. "And her attitude is different. More resigned. In the other pictures, she has more spark."

"And this one?"

"Her eyes are empty and hollow." Fiona turned her head, averting her gaze from the screen. "I saw that same expression on my own face every time I looked in the mirror after Wyatt's death."

"What does it mean?"

"Loss of hope." Slowly, she rose from the table. Her voice dropped to a whisper. "Knowing that you've lost something precious, and you might never find it again."

He came up behind her and gently turned her toward him. "You don't have to hide your tears from me. I understand. I know how much you cared for your husband."

But when she looked, her eyes were dry. "Tennyson said it's better to have loved and lost than never to have loved at all."

She stood so close to him that he could feel the radiant warmth of her body. He sensed the beating of her pulse, the rhythm of her heartbeat. "That's what Tennyson says. But what do *you* say?"

"I'm not a poet."

"But you're an artist."

"Which means I'm *not* good with words. I could draw you a picture."

He didn't need for her to pull out her sketch pad. He could see that she was aware of the chemistry between them. Her lips had parted. Her breathing was shallow.

The fire was there.

The question was: would she fan the flames?

If she wanted him to back off, now would be the time to tell him. "I know you have an opinion about love and passion."

Her eyes invited him to come closer. A gradual smile spread across her face. "I haven't given up on love."

Chapter Eight

While Fiona had been sitting beside him, the dining-room table provided a natural barrier. Now there was nothing but air between her and Jesse. That air was charged with tension and promise.

"You're not wearing the sling anymore," she said.

"I'm feeling a lot stronger."

She could see that was true. He didn't seem like the same man who'd nearly collapsed. "The oatmeal cured you."

"No doubt."

She reached toward his shoulder and lightly touched the bulge of bandages under his blue flannel shirt. "Do you need help changing the dressings?"

Too easily, she imagined peeling away his shirt and gliding her fingers across his bare chest. A rising tide of sudden warmth elevated her temperature. Her skin prickled with sensual awareness that penetrated deeper, causing her blood to race. It had been a very long time since she'd felt this kind of arousal, and she didn't know what to do about it.

"You're blushing," he said.

"Am I?" She pulled her hand back. Fantasizing about him wasn't appropriate. He'd only agreed to stay with her because of an imagined debt to her late husband. She needed to be careful not to misinterpret his kindness as something else.

Jesse glided the back of his hand along her cheek. "I like the color in your face."

Oh, good. Because she felt as if she was turning bright red from the roots of her hair to her toenails. She was glad to realize that it definitely wasn't kindness that emanated from him. "Your eyes."

"What about them?"

"The color is like a glaze I use in pottery. Rich, dark, coffee-brown."

"I'd like to see some of your work."

That should be a cue to take him into her studio. To put some distance between them. But she didn't want to separate. Instead, she leaned closer. The tips of her breasts were mere inches away from his chest. She tilted her chin up.

When their lips met, the teasing warmth became a powerful torrent. She actually felt as if she were being transported, swept away by one gentle kiss. Never before had she experienced anything like this. Excitement rushed through her, leaving her breathless.

Gasping, she stepped backward, out of his

embrace. Looking into his face, she saw her desire reflected. She knew, without a doubt, that this attraction could only end one way. Soon, they would be in each other's arms. Soon, they would be making love. *Am I ready? Is it time?*

Her longing was tempered with panic. She'd never imagined that she'd be able to feel this way. She was a widow with a small child, resigned to a life of responsibility without passion. How could this be happening? "Jesse, I—"

He laid his finger across her lips, stopping her words. "No need to speak."

He was right. These churning emotions required no explanation. She could trust the way she felt and know that he'd felt it, too. For now, that was enough.

"Fiona." His voice caressed her name.

"Yes?"

"I appreciate your offer to change my dressings, but Wentworth will be here soon. He's a medic. He likes messing around with surgical stuff."

She might enjoy messing around, too. *Tell him.* She wanted another kiss. If she let this moment pass, it might not come again. Which was a good reason *not* to tell him. *But it's too soon. And I'm afraid.*

She cleared her throat and took another step back. "I have an ointment that might be soothing. When I'm sculpting, it seems like I'm always getting cuts and burns on my hands."

"Some kind of nontraditional medicine?" he asked.

"I didn't make it myself, but all the ingredients are from nature."

"My grandfather had a remedy for healing, made from creosote bush, prickly pear and some mysterious herb with a Navajo name I can't pronounce." His smile turned nostalgic. "He believed the strongest medicine came from within. Trusting your body to heal itself."

"You've mentioned your grandfather before." She wanted to know more about Jesse. "Tell me about him."

"He lived on the reservation."

She returned to her seat at the table, and he did the same. Though she regretted the distance between them, she was also relieved. With her long-suppressed hormones raging, she wasn't able to think straight. "Did you live there, too?"

"I'm a city kid. We lived in Denver. My mom isn't Navajo, but she wanted me and my sister to know and appreciate our heritage. She sent us to live with our grandparents every summer."

"And was she right? Did you learn to appreciate that life?"

"Probably more than the kids who grew up on the rez. Our time there was limited and special. We were hungry for knowledge, fascinated by the old ways and rituals. And we knew we could always return to our urban life. My sister said we had the best of both worlds."

"Are you close to her?"

"Elena is the office manager for Longbridge Security."

He seemed to be devoted to his family. That was a check mark on the plus side. "You haven't mentioned your father."

"He was in the marines. He died when I was seven. I hardly remember him."

"I'm sorry," Fiona said.

"My mother remarried a couple of years after he died. My stepfather is a good man, a good provider."

His mother—a widow like her—managed to find love again. Not an unusual situation. Lots of people had second chances. There wasn't a rule that said Fiona had to live the rest of her life alone, draped in widow's weeds. She just wasn't accustomed to thinking that way.

"My grandfather," Jesse said quietly, "passed away a few years ago. Sometimes, he seems to be with me."

"I understand. His memory lives through you."

"It's something more," he said. "When I was in the hospital, they said that I died on the operating table for a few minutes. I saw him. My grandfather."

Many people talked about seeing a white light and being reacquainted with others who had passed away. "Did he say anything?"

"He was there to welcome me," Jesse said. "But I wasn't ready to go with him. Not yet. There's something more I need to do with my life."

Had he come back from death to be with her? Were they both being given a second chance? "What is it, Jesse? What do you need to do?"

"I'll wait and see. And trust that I'll recognize the true path when it appears before me."

She wanted to walk beside him on that trail.

No matter where it led. Their brief kiss had been the first step. She could hardly wait to see what came next.

PETE RICHTER WATCHED as the lights inside the widow Grant's house were turned off one by one. From where he was standing in the forest, he couldn't actually see inside because the curtains were pulled. But the glow at the edges of the windows went out until only one lamp in the living room was still lit.

Richter figured the bodyguard would station himself there, near the fireplace. Even though no smoke rose from the chimney, the thought of a warm blaze made him feel even colder. It was below freezing out here. He needed to act soon before he turned into a damn icicle.

The widow's bedroom was at the end of the cabin, far away from the front room. He could break through her window and grab her, but he wouldn't be able to haul her away before her security man responded. It might be smart to kill him first.

But the curtains were drawn. Richter couldn't see to get a clear shot at the son of a bitch who, by all rights, should already have been dead.

Walking carefully so he wouldn't make any noise, he tried to come up with a plan. There had to be a way for him to get to the widow— another way into her house.

He'd find it soon enough. Then he'd make her tell him where she'd hidden his money.

WITH FIONA SAFELY TUCKED into bed, Jesse sat in a wooden rocking chair beside the fireplace with his gun resting on the table beside him. Though he would have been a hell of a lot more comfortable on the sofa, he couldn't allow himself to take off his shoes and relax. If he did that, he'd be asleep in minutes.

Leaning forward with his elbows resting on

his thighs, he listened. Both doors to the bedrooms were ajar, and he could hear Abby and Fiona shifting in their beds. He thought of Fiona's long hair spread across the pillows, and her graceful body stretched out across the sheets. Her face in repose. Her lips.

He hadn't planned to kiss her, but he didn't regret that moment. It tasted right. And the sensual jolt to his system had gotten his heart pumping and his blood circulating. He felt better now than he had since he woke in the hospital. If he made love to her, he'd probably be completely cured.

A sound outside the window interrupted his reverie. The wind rattling the bare branches of the aspens near the front door? He wouldn't take any chances. Gun in hand, he went to the curtains and peered around the edge. From this limited vantage point, he saw nothing suspicious.

One-man guard duty was difficult. If Wentworth had been here, one of them could have gone outside to check while the other stayed here. Alone, he couldn't risk leaving the house unprotected.

He checked his wristwatch. Wentworth was supposed to be here any minute.

He sank into the rocking chair again. Waiting. Listening.

The next sound seemed to come from overhead. A tree squirrel running across the roof? He looked up.

It was quiet again.

Then he heard the tires from Wentworth's vehicle pulling up the gravel drive. He stood at the front door, watching as Wentworth got out of the car, and motioned him inside.

With the door bolted, Jesse said, "I heard something on the roof."

"How big?"

"Don't know. It was a scraping noise."

Wentworth exhaled a weary sigh. It had

been a long day for him, too. "What should we do about it?"

"You stay here. I'll go out and take a look around."

Though Jesse would have preferred using a rifle, his left arm wasn't steady enough to be trusted. He took his handgun and stepped outside. Earlier today, he'd had an opportunity to check out her house from various angles, figuring out which direction an intruder might take. But he hadn't considered the roof.

The cold night air was bracing. After taking a moment to allow his eyes get accustomed to the moonlight, he circled around to the rear of the house. None of the aspens at the front of the house were good for climbing; the branches started too far from the ground. At the back, there was one tall pine tree.

Hc stared into the depths of its branches. Nothing there.

The roof of Fiona's one-story house formed a shallow peak—just enough of an angle to encourage the snow to slide off. He saw nothing in the back or the front. But he sensed a threat.

When he returned to the inside of the house, Wentworth escorted him into the kitchen. "Here's the deal, Jesse. I'll change those dressings. Then you go to bed. I'll wake you in three hours to relieve me."

"You should go back to the Carlisle Ranch."

"They don't need me. Our man, Neville, is there. And Burke. And a whole mob of cowboys with rifles."

Though Jesse didn't like to admit that he needed help, he wasn't a fool. "I won't lie. I could use some rest."

He had the feeling that the next couple of days weren't going to get any easier.

Chapter Nine

By dawn of the following day, Jesse felt damn good. The aching lessened. His drumming headache was gone. He'd recovered a decent range of movement in his arm and shoulder but continued to wear the sling as a reminder to be careful.

Best of all, his appetite had returned. He sat at the table in Fiona's cheery tangerine kitchen, scarfing down the excellent pancakes she'd whipped up. On the other side of the table, Wentworth polished off the last morsel of food on his plate. Fork in hand, he eyed a sausage link on Jesse's plate.

"Don't even think about it," Jesse growled.

"As a medical professional," Wentworth said, "I'd advise you to turn over the meat."

"Based on what diagnosis?"

"Anatomy charts. There's a link-size space in my belly."

"To match the hole in your head," Jesse said. "You're crazy if you think I'm not eating this."

Abby was between them, kneeling on her chair because she was, as she had informed them, too grown-up for a booster seat. Her eating process was complicated. Each bite she took was followed by a bite for her plastic palomino pony. "What are we going to do today?" she asked.

"Mickey is coming over," Fiona said as she slid another pancake from the frying pan onto Wentworth's plate.

"Mickey?" Jesse glanced up at her.

"Abby's friend."

"My best friend," Abby clarified.

Jesse couldn't believe what he was hearing. Fiona had scheduled a playdate? "You'll have to cancel."

"Or not." She was pretty in the morning with her long brown hair pulled back in a ponytail and her cheeks flushed pink from the heat of the stovetop. "Mickey's mom should be dropping him off any minute."

"So early? It's barely light outside."

"Yee-haw," Abby cheered. "I gotta get dressed."

Fiona looked down at her daughter's plate, gave a satisfied nod and said, "You're excused."

Abby hopped off her chair and bolted from the room with her pony tucked under her arm.

Jesse had the distinct feeling that he was losing control of the situation. "This is wrong, Fiona. Wentworth and I are here as bodyguards. Not babysitters."

"Mickey always comes over on Wednesdays

while Belinda works the morning shift at the café. I couldn't ask her to reschedule on such short notice."

He reminded her, "Richter is still at large."

"He's not going to attack while you're here," she said. "Besides, it'll be easier for everyone if Abby's occupied with her friend. Otherwise, she'll be underfoot."

After she shoveled the last pancake onto his plate, Fiona excused herself and went to oversee her daughter.

Jesse cut his sausage in half, looked at Wentworth and shook his head. "A playdate."

"I used to date a single mom," Wentworth said. "There's nothing more sacred than their babysitting schedules."

"Even when you find a dead body in the front yard? Fiona ought to have the good sense to be more cautious."

"That's why she's got you, buddy."

"And you." Jesse shoved the sausage into his

146 Bodyguard Under the Mistletoe

mouth. "I need you here today, instead of at the Carlisle Ranch."

Wentworth carried his plate to the sink. "Have you got a plan?"

"Searching." He envisioned a widening circle. "We'll start here at Fiona's house."

"But we already searched," Wentworth said.

"I need to see for myself. And I want Fiona with me. She might notice something that others missed. Then I want to take a look around at the Circle M where Nicole was held prisoner. After that, I'll check the site where the ransom was dropped. Maybe I can pick up the kidnappers' trail."

"After two days?" Wentworth scoffed. "You're a genius tracker, Jesse. But that's nearly impossible."

"It's a long shot," he agreed. "But we haven't got much to go on."

He heard Abby racing through the house and shouting, "Mickey's here. Mickey's here."

Jesse went to the front door, where Abby tugged at the brace that was holding it shut. She looked up at him. "The door's broke."

"This is a special lock." *A childproof lock.* Though the brace was supposed to keep intruders out, it also ensured that Abby couldn't go racing outside whenever she wanted. An unexpected benefit. "Whenever you want it moved, ask me or your mom or Wentworth."

"Open," she said.

Fiona stood beside them. "Did you hear what Jesse said? For the next few days, you aren't to go outside without permission."

"Yes." Her blond curls flounced as she nodded. "Open."

Fiona opened the door and welcomed her guests. Mickey was a skinny, three-and-a-half-foot tall bundle of energy with a buzz haircut and freckles. He threw off his jacket and ran down the hallway behind Abby.

His mother had a nicely rounded figure. Her

full hips were packed into black slacks. The fringe on her leather jacket jiggled when she moved.

"Belinda Miller," Fiona said, "this is Jesse Longbridge and Tom Wentworth."

Though her smile was dimpled and friendly when she shook hands, he saw caution in her brown eyes. Belinda couldn't have been more than twenty-five years old, but she'd already learned to be wary of men. From what Jesse had read in Burke's reports, her ex-husband had a nasty temper.

"Tell me the truth," she said. "Is there any real danger?"

As Jesse said, "Yes," Fiona said, "Not really."

Belinda planted her fists on her hips. "Which is it?"

"Even if there is somebody after us," Fiona said, "these two men are professional body-guards."

Belinda's gaze assessed him and Wentworth;

then she gave a satisfied nod. "Nobody is going to mess with you guys."

Fiona gave her a hug. "See you after lunch."

"Thanks, hon. I really need this shift. It's almost Christmas, and I'm dead broke."

He watched Belinda return to her car and drive away. The morning skies grew brighter. It was a new day. When he returned to the house and locked the door, he was warm. Comfortable. His belly full of good food.

At the far end of the hallway, he heard the kids playing. Fiona smiled at him, and he fought the urge to give her a little peck on the forehead. *This must be what it's like to have a family.*

He seldom considered the idea of having a family of his own. Bodyguards needed to look on the dark side, to recognize potential threats before they became lethal. If he had his own family, there was also the possibility that he might lose them.

But when he looked around this comfortable

cabin, he felt content. He wouldn't have minded starting a fire in the hearth and spending the whole day playing with the kids and gazing into Fiona's soft gray eyes. Maybe read a book. He remembered a December, long ago, when he had whittled kachina dolls for Christmas presents. Whittling was a good hobby. He should take it up again.

Yeah, right. Then he could have some hot chocolate with marshmallows. Coming back from death might have mellowed him, but he wasn't about to turn into a lazy, domesticated tomcat. Clearing his throat, Jesse took command and issued orders. "We need to get started. Wentworth, you stay here with the kids. Fiona, come with me to search."

Someday, there might be time for whittling and reveries in front of the fireplace. But not today.

FIONA ZIPPED HER WINTER parka all the way to her chin as she led Jesse to the structure nearest the house. "This was going to be my art studio. Wyatt never had a chance to finish it."

They went up two steps and entered through the unlocked double-wide door. The single room was two stories high at the front with large windows to admit natural light. The ceiling slanted down to a single story at the rear. Except for a couple of sawhorses and a stack of two-by-fours, the room was empty.

Jesse strode across the wood floor. His footsteps echoed. He stopped at the rear where there was a section of concrete. "You'd put the kiln here."

"Right. This whole building rests on a concrete slab. You wouldn't believe how much Wyatt enjoyed that part of the construction. He got to use a backhoe."

"Heavy equipment," Jesse said with obvious relish. "Yeah, that's fun stuff."

"A lot of the men in the Grant family seem to think so. Most of them are professionals who sit at a desk all day. But when they come up here—supposedly to relax—they take on building projects."

"It's satisfying to create something solid." Jesse rested his hand against an exposed stud on the framed wall. "Wouldn't take much to finish this. Add the insulation and the drywall."

"And the electric," she reminded him. "And minimal plumbing. I don't need a toilet, but I'd like a sink. And a tile floor so it would be easy to clean up."

He removed his hand. "A bigger job than I thought."

"I've had Belinda's ex-husband out here to give me an estimate on finishing. Nate's a handyman, and he's pretty good."

"I saw in Burke's investigation notes that he was a suspect in Nicole's kidnapping."

Fiona wasn't surprised. Nate was an efficient worker, but she didn't have a high opinion of his character. "He hates the Carlisles and blames them for losing his ranch."

"Any truth to his opinion?"

"It's an old grudge. Years ago, when Carolyn's father changed his ranching procedures to all-organic with grass-fed cattle and no antibiotics, everybody thought he was nuts. Organic beef is more expensive to raise, and involves a lot more effort. But old Sterling Carlisle knew what he was doing. Carlisle Certified Organic Beef grew into a multimillion-dollar international success story."

"And Nate lost almost everything."

"I think it was his father who told Sterling Carlisle to go to hell when he offered to buy Circle M cattle if they made the required changes in ranching procedures. The Circle M became less and less profitable. Nate finally closed down the cattle ranch and sold off some of his land. He was lucky when the Sons of Freedom rented his property."

Jesse scowled. "Given that he's not a particularly charming individual, why did you hire him?"

"Indirectly, I was helping Belinda. If her ex-husband has money, he can pay his child support."

"Anything else?"

"I guess, in a way, I feel sorry for Nate. He was terrible to Belinda. When they were first separated, he pestered her until she took out a restraining order. But he adores Mickey. When he's with his son, he lights up."

"You like to find the good in people. Even when you have to look deep."

"It's my greatest flaw."

Her positive attitude had certainly betrayed her. Instead of seeing how Wyatt's first wife and grown children would greedily gobble up every asset they could get their sticky fingers on, she believed they were—like her—grieving his death and wishing her the best. Had she made a similar mistake with Nate Miller?

Jesse stamped his foot on the floor again and listened to the echo. "Is there a basement under here?"

"Just a crawl space. It's probably only three feet high."

"Big enough to hide the ransom," he said. "We'll need a flashlight."

"There's one in the barn. I'll get it."

"Fiona, wait. You shouldn't be alone."

"Don't worry. I know exactly where the flashlight is. I'll be right back."

She darted out the door and jogged across the yard toward the old barn with a stable in back. She hadn't been in here recently. Since they weren't keeping livestock, there wasn't a need to visit the barn.

She opened the small door on the side and slipped inside. It smelled stale and stuffy. This old, empty building reminded her of how much she'd lost. It'd take a miracle for her to get Abby the pony she wanted so much.

She flicked the light switch. None of the lights came on. The bulbs must be burned out.

It didn't matter. The light from the door and the two high windows was enough for her to see. She carefully picked her way through the junk stored in the central area below the loft: a space heater that didn't work, camping supplies, an ancient tractor, a Jeep with a snowplow attached to the front.

Near the tool bench were several metal boxes where Wyatt had stored his tools when he wasn't using them. Some of the lids stood open. When Burke and the deputies searched last night, they must have dug through here. She was glad that others had been the first to search. They probably knocked away most of the cobwebs.

She reached toward the dusty shelf above the workbench and found a heavy-duty silver flashlight. She'd purchased it herself because it had a specially designed reflection system and a fancy battery that was supposed to last for years and years. True to that guarantee, a strong, steady beam shot through the musty air as soon as she touched the switch. She moved the flashlight back and forth; the light scanned across the discarded equipment and the muddy footprints on the wood floor. The old wood creaked beneath her sneakers.

She sensed that she wasn't alone.

Shadows seemed to take solid form. From the loft overhead, she heard a scuffling noise. She aimed the beam at the rough wooden staircase leading to the loft. What if Richter came charging down those stairs?

She'd be a fool to stand here and wait for him. Gathering her courage, she ran for the door and burst outside into the fresh sunlight.

Jesse was walking toward her. He immediately picked up on her mood. "What's wrong?"

"It's nothing." Only an overactive imagination. She held up the flashlight. "Found it."

"If you saw something, Fiona, you need to

tell me. Anything out of the ordinary might be a threat. Or a clue."

"I got spooked." She shrugged. "The barn is kind of creepy with all that old discarded equipment. I should just get rid of it all."

"You could sell it."

The thought hadn't occurred to her, but it was a good idea. "You're absolutely right. There might be someone who'd pay for a broken-down snowplow."

"That's a project for another day." He took the flashlight from her. "Let's see what's under the studio."

Inside, he'd found an access point—a trapdoor that he'd already opened. Jesse took off his cowboy hat and slipped his arm out of the sling.

She watched as he climbed down into the crawl space and disappeared. Peeking down, she saw the flashlight beam slashing through the darkness. She asked, "Do you see anything?"

"Boards and braces. Nice solid construction."

She stroked the brim of his hat. The dark brown felt was weathered but not worn-out. Tied around the crown was a leather thong with two turquoise beads at the end. Another totem? She recalled the small pouch he carried in his pocket and smiled. Even a bodyguard like Jesse felt the need for reassurance and protection.

He emerged from the hole. "Nothing down there. Not even a raccoon's nest."

"Too bad. I was hoping for a quick solution."

Instead, they could cross this building off their list of places to search. Jesse raked his hair off his forehead and slapped his hat back onto his head. "Next, the barn."

Halfway across the backyard, he paused and looked past the house toward the driveway. Following his gaze, Fiona saw a truck approaching her house. "It's Nate Miller."

"Any reason for him to be here?"

"None at all."

Chapter Ten

Jesse hustled toward the front of the house, coming around the corner in time to confront Nate Miller as he left his truck. "Can I help you?"

Nate squinted under his battered flat-brim hat. The skin on his pointed jaw was red and nicked as if he'd shaved with a dull razor. His clothes were clean, and his jeans were ironed with a crease down the front. It appeared that he was trying to make a good impression. For Fiona? Did the handyman have a crush on her?

Unsmiling, he stuck out his hand. "Don't believe we've met. I'm Nate Miller."

Jesse accepted the handshake. "Jesse Longbridge."

"You're the fella who got shot. The security man. Glad to see you up and around."

Though Nate had offered proper condolence, his tone was offhand and insincere. He had something else on his mind, which didn't matter to Jesse because he had an agenda of his own. He wanted to take a look around at the Circle M, and that property belonged to Nate.

Fiona joined them. "Hi, Nate. Jesse is staying with us until this trouble is over."

"I suppose that's a good thing. A young woman like you shouldn't be alone when there are dangerous men on the loose."

His comment might have implied an interest in her, but Jesse didn't get that sense. Nate's gaze darted nervously; he barely noticed Fiona.

"Thanks for your concern," she said. "Did we have an appointment?"

"Nope. I was just thinking that maybe I could take Mickey off your hands. For an hour or so."

As soon as he mentioned his son's name, Jesse understood why Nate had cleaned himself up and shaved. He was on his best behavior— anxious to show Fiona that he was trustworthy, capable of taking care of his son.

Nate continued. "Since Logan and his people got arrested, the Circle M belongs to me again. I got eight horses that belonged to Logan. I'm paying to board those animals, and I figure they might belong to me pretty soon. I bet Mickey would like to see those ponies. And Abby, too."

"That's very thoughtful," Fiona said. "Have you okayed this plan with Belinda?"

"She won't mind." A note of anger tainted his voice. "We don't need to bother telling her."

"No bother." Fiona pulled her cell phone from

her jacket pocket. "I'll just call the café and make sure that—"

"Don't bother."

As Nate's hand shot out to stop Fiona from punching in the phone number, Jesse reacted. He caught Nate's wrist midair and gave a sharp twist, spinning him around.

Nate recovered his balance. A sneer curled his lower lip. Underneath his veneer of polite behavior, he was angry. "I didn't mean any harm."

"I know." Jesse had positioned himself in front of Fiona, protecting her from Nate's hostility while she called his ex-wife. "If I thought you'd meant to hurt her, you wouldn't be standing."

"You're pretty damn sure of yourself."

"With good reason." Jesse wasn't bragging, just stating the truth. He was a trained protector. Even with a bum shoulder, he could handle Nate Miller. "You share custody with your ex-wife?"

"That's right. I usually have Mickey on weekends. But not this last one. Belinda took him into Grand Junction to stay with her parents overnight." He hooked his thumbs in his belt. "The way I figure, I should have some extra time today. Belinda owes me."

"It must be hard. Being separated from your son."

"Damn right. Mickey needs to be with me. A growing boy needs his father's influence. Know what I mean? I should be showing him how to do chores, how to fish, how to hunt."

"Hunting? He's only four."

"You can't start too soon. I was helping my pappy brand steer when I was only six. It's my God-given right to show my son these things. My right, damn it."

He was bitter, anxious and a little bit obsessive. Though Fiona thought Nate was a good parent, Jesse saw a darker side to this possessiveness. He wondered how far Nate would go to be with his son.

He tucked that concern into the ever-expanding

puzzle surrounding Nicole's kidnapping. "I suppose you've heard about the missing ransom."

"You bet I have. That's one of the reasons I moved back to the Circle M as soon as the sheriff's men gave the okay."

"Have you been searching?"

He gave a sly nod. "A million dollars would change my life."

"You'd have to return the money," Jesse said.

"Finders, keepers. The Carlisles already have too much damn cash. Dylan wouldn't miss a million. That's chump change to him."

That wasn't the way the law saw it, but Jesse didn't bother pointing that out. He wanted Nate's cooperation. "I'd like to take a look around at the Circle M."

Nate's jaw tightened. Offering hospitality didn't come naturally to him. "I suppose it would be all right. Just don't bring any of those damn Carlisles with you."

Fiona rejoined them. "Belinda says thanks

but no, thanks. She's a little concerned that Mickey might be getting an ear infection so she wanted him to stay inside."

"She's coddling the boy. Turning him into a sissy."

"Hold on, Nate." When Fiona touched his arm, he barely kept himself from flinching. "Belinda said she'd stop by the Circle M with Mickey when her shift is over."

"Fine. I'll be waiting."

He turned on his boot heel and went back to his truck. Jesse watched as he drove away. "That's one angry man."

"But you see what I mean? He's crazy about his son."

Crazy *being the relevent word,* thought Jesse.

AFTER NATE'S SURPRISE VISIT, Fiona wanted to check in with Wentworth and the kids before they did any further searching. If Mickey had noticed his father's truck, he might have questions.

On the phone, Belinda had been adamant about refusing to let Nate take the kids. She'd argued with her ex-husband about the weekend visit to her parents, which had actually been a chance for her mom and dad to meet her new boyfriend. He and Belinda had been living together for six months, and marriage was in their future. Another bone of contention with Nate.

Wentworth opened the door, wearing a tinfoil crown.

"Nice hat," Jesse commented as he entered.

"I'm the king," Wentworth said. "King of the Wild Prairie. And these are my two ponies."

Abby and Mickey trotted toward them, bobbing their heads and making whinnying noises.

Fiona chuckled. "What wonderful steeds!"

Mickey bared his teeth and snapped at her fingers. Apparently, he was a carnivorous breed of horse.

"Here's the magic part," Wentworth said. "I pat them on the head. Poof. They turn into kids."

Playing the game, Abby immediately dropped the horse act and gave Fiona a hug. "Where were you, Mommy?"

"Jesse and I were out back, looking around."

"Looking for what?"

Fiona squatted so she was eye level with her daughter. No way would she frighten Abby with stories of kidnapping and ransom. Neither would she lie. Picking her words carefully, she said, "There might be something hidden on our property. It's about as big as that coffee table."

A frown puckered Abby's forehead. "Is it in a secret hiding place?"

Fiona realized that she might be encouraging her daughter to go on a treasure hunt. That was the last thing she wanted. "This is a grown-up problem. Jesse and I will take care of it."

Abby glanced toward Jesse, then back at her mother. She seemed unconvinced. "What if you can't find it? What if you need me and Mickey to find the secret place?"

Did she know about the ransom? A chill crept up Fiona's spine. She hated to think of her daughter being connected in any way to these horrible crimes. "Is there something you want to tell me?"

Mickey whinnied and pawed the air with his hands.

"Got to run," Abby said. "Run like the wind."

As her daughter galloped down the hall with Mickey at her side, Fiona rose slowly. "She knows something."

"She does," Jesse agreed. "Mickey, too."

Abby had immediately mentioned a secret hiding place. Usually, she and Mickey were outside, racing around. It was entirely possible that they'd discovered many things that Fiona knew nothing about, including some kind of hidey-hole.

Convincing her daughter to open up wouldn't be easy. Abby could be intensely stubborn.

"I'll talk to her," Jesse offered.

She raised a skeptical eyebrow. "Why would she tell you if she won't talk to me?"

"You're her mother. Abby's secret might get her in trouble with you, and she doesn't want that. On the other hand, I'm just some guy who gave her a turquoise stone. No threat."

Fiona certainly didn't see him as nonthreatening. The way he'd manhandled Nate in the front yard had been quick, efficient and a little bit scary.

And there was an even greater threat. Jesse knew how to shatter the wall she'd built around her heart to protect herself. When he looked at her with those deep-set eyes, she had the urge to unburden all the thoughts and emotions she usually held back. Within an hour of meeting him, she'd confided details about her financial situation that she hadn't told anyone else. Last night, they were even more intimate. After knowing him for less than a day, she'd been kissing him. Oh, yes, he was dangerous. A huge threat to her self-control.

But she was certain that he didn't mean to hurt her or her daughter.

"Go ahead and talk to Abby." She turned to Wentworth. "So, Your Royal Highness, how about a cup of coffee?"

"If you're buying, I'm drinking."

He followed her into the kitchen, removed his crown and sat in the same chair he'd used for breakfast. He rested his elbows on the tabletop as she poured two cups. Remembering that he took his with milk and sugar, she placed both on the table within easy reach.

"Have the kids been driving you crazy?" she asked.

"Playing king is a whole lot more fun than hanging around in the hospital waiting for Jesse to wake up."

"He seems to be recovering quickly."

Wentworth stirred the milk into his coffee. "It takes more than dying to keep Jesse down."

She didn't like to think of Jesse dying, being

summoned to the hereafter by his grandfather. After one sip of coffee, she set her mug down on the table. "If you don't mind, I should get these dishes done before it's time to make lunch."

They'd never installed a dishwasher at the cabin. Though they had a good well, water was a precious commodity in the Colorado mountains, and she tried to practice conservation, teaching Abby about the three *R*s. Reduce. Reuse. Recycle.

One half of the double sink filled with sudsy water. The other half was for rinsing.

"How long have you been working for Jesse?" she asked.

"Almost five years. And I've known him since high school in Denver. He was a couple of years older and didn't pay much attention to me back then. I was friends with his younger sister, Elena."

"The office manager for Longbridge Security," she recalled. "Is she like Jesse?"

"Oh, yeah. She's tough, and she's smart.

Went to law school and passed the bar exam on her first try."

"I know a lot of attorneys in Denver."

"Elena's more than a lawyer. She's an excellent markswoman. And she can kick my ass in hand-to-hand combat."

"Tough and smart." Fiona was intrigued by the idea of a female version of Jesse. "How else is she like her brother?"

"They both like to be the boss. It makes things real interesting when they're together."

His grin made her think that he cared about Elena. "Is she your girlfriend?"

The smile wilted. "Just friends."

"Don't give up on her." Fiona turned back to the dishes. "It takes some women a while to get warmed up. Relationships happen in all kinds of surprising ways."

Like the feelings she had for Jesse. The electricity that raced through her when they touched. Her fascination with his chiseled features. If anyone had told her that she'd move to an isolated mountain home and find a man who attracted her, she wouldn't have believed them.

She glanced toward the kitchen door. "Why do you think it's taking Jesse so long?"

"Interrogations take time."

"Interrogation? He's not going to pressure my daughter, is he?"

"Don't worry. Abby will be fine. She's a persuasive kid. Hell, she got me to wear a crown and play king."

Jesse strode into the kitchen and came up close beside her. In a low voice, he said, "You have to promise that you won't be mad at Abby."

Was her daughter in danger? A tremor raced through her, and she placed the last dish in the rack on the counter to dry. "What has Abby done?"

"She broke one of your rules, and she's scared that you'll be angry."

She turned to face him. "Which rule?"

"First, you have to promise."

Her imagination ran through all the potentially dangerous situations her daughter could have gotten into. "I promise."

"When you first moved up here, Abby and Mickey were playing outside. They went exploring in the barn."

"She knows better than that. I've told her a hundred times not to go into any of the outbuildings. It's not safe. There are—"

"You promised," he reminded her.

"Fine." Her lips pinched together. "What did the kids find?"

"A secret playhouse under the floorboards. They only went in there a couple of times. They accidentally left the lights on in the barn and the bulbs must have burned out."

"A playhouse?" She rested her hand on her chest. Her heart fluttered as she thought of all the terrible things that might have happened.

"You've never heard of this before?"

She shook her head. "Never. But it's entirely possible that one of the Grant men built something like that as a weekend project. Maybe a root cellar?"

But why would anyone put a root cellar in the barn? She needed to see this secret playhouse.

After giving Abby a hug and assuring her that she was a much-loved child who should never, under any circumstance, go exploring without telling her mother first, Fiona followed Jesse to the barn.

Though they had the flashlight, Jesse opened the two wide doors at the front. Sunlight flooded into the barn, banishing the ominous dark. He picked his way through the discarded junk that had taken up residence.

Fiona saw every bit of this stuff—the tractor, the Jeep and the beat-up boxes of junk—as potential hazards. Abby and Mickey could have seriously injured themselves while playing in here.

"Wouldn't Burke or the sheriff have found

this playhouse?" she asked. "They searched all over the barn."

"You'd think so," he said. "According to Abby's directions the playhouse is in this corner. On the other side of the barn from the workbench."

Tucked into that corner was a stack of logs covered by a tarp. Jesse shone the flashlight on the floorboards. "You can see footprints here. They searched in this area."

"I don't see a trapdoor."

"It's hidden under the wood," he said. "Abby said that when she and Mickey found it, the door was already open."

"Somebody was in here. They hid the entrance."

He removed the chunks of firewood, revealing a spot on the floor that was swept clean. Even though they knew what to look for, the latch wasn't noticeable. Jesse pulled up the trapdoor.

He shone the flashlight into a dark space. "Maybe you should stay up here."

"Not a chance." She needed to know what was down there, what had been hidden on her property.

Jesse climbed down a short ladder, and she followed.

After a moment of fumbling around, he turned on a lamp.

She stood in a small room, less than ten feet square. The floor was packed earth covered by two threadbare carpets. The ceiling was only six feet high—too low for Jesse to stand upright. The ceiling was insulated, as were the walls, and it was warm.

There was a single bed, a table and a lamp.

Jesse's eyes were grim. "I think we've found the place where Nicole was held prisoner."

Chapter Eleven

Richter lay flat on the floor of the hay loft in the barn, peeking down through a crack between the boards, watching the widow and her bodyguard as they opened the trapdoor hidden under a pile of wood.

His gun was cocked and ready. If they climbed out of that secret hiding place toting the ransom, he'd kill them both.

How the hell had he missed that trapdoor? He'd been all over this damn barn. He'd even pulled logs off the woodpile, thinking the ransom could have been tucked underneath.

She'd known. Fiona must have known.

The more Richter thought about it, the more he was convinced that she and Butch had a thing going on. She must have shown him the hiding spot.

He licked his lips, anticipating the moment when she'd shove a big, fat bundle of cash out of that hole onto the floor of the barn. He'd wait until they both climbed out and were patting each other on the back, congratulating themselves for getting their mitts on that money.

Richter figured he'd shoot the bodyguard first. He should've made sure he killed that guy before. Three bullets weren't enough to stop him. This time, he'd go for a clean head shot. At this range, he couldn't miss.

Fiona climbed out first. Her long hair wasn't braided today, and her ponytail tangled around her shoulders. She stood below him, brushing the dust off her hands.

The bodyguard climbed up beside her.

Richter's trigger finger twitched.

But the bodyguard's hands were empty. He didn't have the ransom.

"I never knew that little room was there," Fiona said. "Do you think it was meant to be a playhouse?"

The bodyguard slapped his hat back onto his head. "I think someone was living there. An adult."

"Why?"

"It's set up nice and cozy with a bed and a lamp. The furniture has been there long enough to make marks on the floor. There's even electricity."

"But why would anyone want to live there?"

He shrugged. "We need to call the sheriff. There might be fingerprints."

As they walked toward the open door of the

barn, Fiona shook her head. "Too bad the ransom wasn't stashed in there."

Richter eased up on the trigger. It was too bad *for him* that they hadn't found the ransom, but lucky for *them*. The widow and her bodyguard would live to see another day.

FIONA STAYED IN THE house with the kids while Jesse and a herd of law enforcement people inspected the small room under the floorboards in the barn. Though unaccustomed to having so many visitors at her mountain home, she'd been a political wife long enough to know the rules of proper hospitality. *Offer them something to eat and make a fresh pot of coffee.* She whipped up a chocolate cakc from a mix.

Drawn by the sweet aroma of baking, Abby and Mickey appeared in the kitchen door. Abby's little face crinkled with worry. "Mommy, are you mad at me?"

"Not mad. Just worried." She pulled her

daughter into a hug. "You know I always love you."

"Love you back."

"You did the right thing by telling Jesse about the secret place. You can always tell me anything. You know that, don't you?"

Abby nodded. "Can we go out to the barn and say hi to everybody?"

"No," Fiona said, firm and final. The sheriff and his deputies would be annoyed by kids underfoot. But more important, she wanted to shield the children from all the fearful events surrounding Nicole's kidnapping.

Abby tilted her head to one side. "Can we have cake for lunch?"

"If you finish your fruit and sandwich, you get chocolate cake for dessert."

"I'm hungry," Mickey said in plaintive tone. "Now."

"Fifteen minutes until lunch." She'd set up drawing projects on the dining-room table.

"First, I want you both to make me a picture of Christmas."

They dashed off. She barely had time to swirl frosting across the sheet cake when there was a knock on the back door. Since she'd been told in no uncertain terms to use the dead bolt at all times, Fiona had to flip the lock before opening the door.

Carolyn charged inside, talking as she came. "She was there, right there under your barn. Can you believe it? We had helicopters searching and bloodhounds and—"

"I want to hear everything," Fiona said, "but quietly. I don't want to scare the kids."

"Right." Carolyn lowered her voice to a whisper. "They've found several blond hairs that surely belong to Nicole. And she scratched her initials into the wood near the door. So close. She was so close."

Jesse came into the house and shut the door. "Fiona, they need you at the barn. To take a closer look and see if you can identify any of the furniture or bed linens."

"Sure, no problem." She turned to Carolyn. "I feel terrible that Nicole was held here. Like you said, she was so close. If I'd gone out to the barn, I would have heard her. I could have helped her."

"You're not the only one who feels like she should have done more." Carolyn's fist clenched as if grabbing a missed opportunity. "At the very beginning of all this, I could have stopped Nicole from riding off by herself."

There was plenty of reproach to be spread around. "You're not to blame."

"I know you're right. But why do I feel so guilty?"

Intuitively, she knew the answer. But it was difficult to put into words.

When her husband died from a heart attack, she had tried her hardest to figure out why it happened. She needed a reason, needed to make sense of the tragedy. It had to be somebody's fault. She'd blamed his doctors for not catching the warning signs, blamed his coworkers for not responding quickly enough, but mostly she'd blamed herself for not taking care of him properly.

"Much of what happens in life is beyond our control," she said. "We can regret what happened to Nicole. Or be angry about it. But the kidnapping wasn't our fault."

"I'm not in control?" Carolyn frowned. "I don't much like that idea."

Of course not. She was a CEO who took her responsibilities seriously. "Do you feel guilty about the bad weather when it snows?"

"No."

"Or when the Broncos lost last weekend?"

"Definitely not my fault," Carolyn said. "I used to think if I wore orange underwear, they'd win. Not true."

"So you regret the loss. But don't feel guilty."

Abby and Mickey raced into the kitchen, waving crayon drawings of Santa and reindeer. In unison, they shouted, "Lunch, lunch. Munch, munch."

"I'll take care of these two," Carolyn said. "What should I feed them?"

"Sandwiches. The fixings are in the fridge."

"Dijon? Maybe Brie?"

"They're children, Carolyn. Mayo and cold cuts are fine."

Fiona grabbed her coat from the peg by the door and walked with Jesse toward the barn.

"I liked what you said about guilt. Wise words."

Never before had anyone accused her of wisdom. It felt a bit uncomfortable. "Life's too short to waste time feeling guilty. I just go with the flow."

"Do you?"

"Like the California girl I am." She pantomimed surfing. "Wherever the waves take me, I go."

And the current of her emotions was sweeping her inexorably toward him. Ahead of them—in the barn—several law enforcement officers were working hard to find clues. Behind them—in the house—her daughter demanded attention and reassurance. But when she was with Jesse, everything else faded into the background. His presence commanded her full concentration. She liked that feeling, liked how she felt when she was near him.

"There was a time," he said, "when I had a situation that turned out wrong. It was bad, real bad. I blamed myself. The guilt nearly did me in."

"It helps to talk about things that hurt," she said.

"Maybe later." He forced a smile. "The sheriff is waiting."

When she looked toward the barn, she saw Sheriff Trainer with his arms folded across his chest and a cigarette dangling from the corner of his mouth. "I'm not a fan of tobacco, but that man looks like he needs a smoke."

"He's ticked off at himself. His trained forensic people haven't found much, and it took a lead from a couple of four-year-olds to locate the secret room."

As she approached, Fiona smiled, hoping that an offer of cake and coffee would make the sheriff feel better. "Good afternoon, Sheriff. If you'd like a snack—"

"Not now." He stubbed out his cigarette. "Why didn't you tell me about this secret room?"

Taken aback, she said, "Because I didn't know."

"This is your property. Your barn. How is it possible that you didn't know?"

She had several logical reasons: she never went into the barn, wasn't here when it was constructed, had no reason to suspect a hideout. But she refused to dignify his question with an explanation. It was absurd to think that she'd been concealing evidence from the police. "Is there a reason you wanted me to come out here?"

His mouth puckered as if sucking through a thin straw. "Nicole Carlisle was held captive in your barn. The dead body of Butch Thurman was found in your front yard. Hell, you found him."

No cake for you. "It almost sounds like you're accusing me."

"I don't believe in coincidence, Fiona. You're in the center of this mess. And I want to know why."

In the past, she might have politely demurred, hoping that someone else, like Jesse, would step up and fight her battles. But she needed to stand up for herself. "Don't blame me."

"Why shouldn't I?"

"Your men searched in the barn. They couldn't find the trapdoor."

"What's your point?"

Aggression didn't come naturally to her, but she pushed back at him with an accusation of her own. "Maybe your own men missed finding the secret room on purpose. They might be the ones with something to hide."

Agent Burke emerged from the barn and waved to her. "In here, Fiona."

Grateful for Burke's timely summons, she brushed past the sheriff.

Jesse leaned close to her ear and whispered, "Nice job, surfer girl."

"I was rude," she said.

"He deserved it."

For the second time that day, she climbed down into the secret room. Burke and Jesse followed. Both men had to duck to keep from hitting their heads on the low plywood ceiling.

The extra-large Agent Burke looked especially cramped in the small space. "Take a careful look around, Fiona. Tell me if any of the furnishings look familiar."

"Why?"

"This stuff came from somewhere. If we find

the original owner, we might figure out who built this room."

She reached up and touched the ceiling. "This looks like plywood that was being used to build my studio. I can't really tell if it's part of that load or not, but we had plenty of wood and insulation lying around. I have invoices somewhere."

"When was that construction taking place?"

"Three years ago."

Only three years ago? She swallowed hard, uncomfortable with the idea that some unknown person had built a secret hideout in her barn so recently. They'd had plenty of opportunity. Before she moved up here, the property had been vacant, except for when Belinda lived here.

"What about the furniture?" Burke asked.

The single bed had a painted metal frame with rails—unlike anything in the house. There was a bedside table with a drawer and a shelf made of particleboard covered with a wood veneer. "I'm pretty sure that the Grant family never owned such inexpensive furniture."

On the edge of the frame at the foot of the bed was a ragged scar where the paint had been scratched away. She touched the mark.

"We think a chain was fastened there," Burke said.

Fiona shivered. "She was chaincd to the bed?"

"A long chain. It gave her a fair amount of mobility." He pointed to Nicole's initials carved into the wall near the ladder. "She could reach this far. I think he was trying to make her comfortable."

Fiona shuddered. "By confining her?"

"As prisons go, this is a Hilton." Jesse pointed to the lamp on the table. "There was light. The bed isn't bad. And this whole place is insulated so it's warm."

"He gave her clean clothes," Burke added.

"In the proof-of-life videos," Jesse said, "Nicole didn't appear to be suffering."

194 Bodyguard Under the Mistletoe

Fiona knew better. She knew Nicole was putting on an act to keep others from worrying. For someone like her neighbor, a woman who loved the outdoors, not being able to see the sun and feel the wind would be torture. Fiona had only been in here for a few minutes, and it already felt as if the walls were closing in on her.

"There's nothing I can tell you about these furnishings."

"Here's what I don't understand," Jesse said. "In those proof-of-life tapes, Nicole made signals that pointed toward the Circle M Ranch. Did she think she was there?"

Burke shifted his shoulders. His huge body seemed to take up all the space in the room. "Here's the sequence of events as we know them—she was kidnapped at the creek and taken to the Circle M. Then Butch and Richter took her. They went to a cave on the Indian Trail. Then she was here."

"Not the Circle M," Jesse repeated. "Why would she point you in that direction?"

"She could have been drugged when she was brought here. If all she'd seen was the Circle M, she'd assume she was there."

Fiona's gaze fixed on the rough wooden ladder leading out of the room. Imagined echoes of Nicole's suffering rang in her ears. It was hot in here; a light sweat coated her forehead.

"We need to figure out who built this little cubbyhole," Jesse said. "If it wasn't Butch or Richter, someone else might be involved in the kidnapping."

"Sam Logan," Burke said. "You identified him from the mug shots."

"You think he built this place?"

Burke considered for a long moment before shaking his head. "Secret hideouts aren't Logan's style. He likes attention."

"Who else?"

"Me," Fiona said. She couldn't stay here for

one more minute. She reached for the wooden ladder. "Sheriff Trainer seems to think so."

She climbed out of the hole into the cluttered barn. Ridding herself of suspicion was going to take more than going with the flow. Her laissez-faire attitude needed to change.

Jesse came up behind her, rested his hand on her shoulder. "I don't suspect you."

"But others do." She gulped down the musty air of the barn, which tasted wonderful compared to the closed room. "How am I going to prove them wrong? I'm not an investigator. Or a hunter."

"I am." His dark eyes were steady and confident. "Trust me."

She had no other choice.

Chapter Twelve

Sitting on a porch bench at the Circle M ranch house, Jesse waved goodbye to Fiona, Belinda and the kids, who were being escorted across the grounds toward the horse barn by a proprietary Nate Miller. Still dressed in his clean, pressed blue jeans, Nate lectured them about how the Circle M had once been the finest cattle ranch in the valley—a boast that was wide open to debate. From what Jesse understood, the Carlisles always had more land, more cattle and more influence.

Nate had reclaimed the Circle M with a vengeance. The yellow crime scene tape that marked the violence of two days ago had been torn down and stuffed into a bin beside the porch.

According to Burke, Nate had arrived at the Circle M shortly after the Sons of Freedom were taken into custody and wasted no time in stating his claim. It was his legal right to move back to the Circle M when the premises were vacated. Burke said there had been some concern about the ownership of the SOF horses, but the FBI was willing to leave that issue for the local authorities to settle.

Nate glanced over his shoulder at Jesse, who remained seated. He wanted a chance to search the premises without Nate hanging over his shoulder, so he'd told them he was tired, still recovering from his wounds.

Much to his surprise, Fiona had backed up his claim with a vivid description of his injuries, even though she hadn't seen a single scar. She talked about "oozing pus" and "too many stitches to count." Her willingness to lie worried him. Though he didn't believe Sheriff Trainer's suspicions, his only proof to the contrary was his belief in her honesty. He knew he wasn't making a mistake by trusting her. Still…

As soon as they all disappeared into the barn, Jesse left the porch. Though it was a long shot, he hoped to find evidence that Nicolc had been here. In the proof-of-life videos, she signaled clues that pointed to the Circle M. He wanted to find an indication of where she'd gone.

Jesse circled behind the ranch house. Across the open yard were a couple of sheds and a smokehouse for curing beef and venison. He took a quick look inside these smaller structures on his way to the main bunkhouse—a long, low building with several windows covered over with heavy plastic to protect against the winter cold. The door was unlocked.

He stepped inside, turned on the light and entered an open room with two long tables.

Near the entrance, there was a wood-burning stove and a podium. This must have been where Sam Logan preached to his survivalist congregation. Twelve men, eleven women and four children. There was nothing spiritual about this organization. The women had been picked up from the street, promised shelter and drugged into submission. The men had been getting rich from a smuggling scheme.

When the FBI raided the place, it must have been just after dinner. Dirty plates still littered the tables along with half-filled water glasses and mugs filled with congealed coffee. A scrawny Christmas tree stood in the corner, half draped with tinsel. Other decorations were scattered about.

Jesse noticed a doll on the bench by the table. A toy truck overturned over on the floor. A couple of aprons tossed carelessly aside.

Life, interrupted.

He went through a door at the back of the

room, entering a hallway with four closed doors on either side. He opened the first door and found a small room with a bed and dresser. Two simple dresses hung from an open rack. On the dresser was a cheap wristwatch, a hair-brush and an economy-size bottle of mois-turizer beside a stack of fashion magazines. This woman might have been living the simple life, but she dreamed of sequins.

Immediately, Jesse noted that the metal frame on the bed matched the bed found in the secret room under Fiona's barn. If Richter or Butch had constructed that room, it seemed likely that they'd use furnishings from the Circle M.

This connection needed further investigation. He quickly checked the rest of the rooms, searching for clues. Where was Nicole now? He didn't think she'd run off with Richter, a man with a criminal record and a mean streak. Had she simply collected the ransom and ridden off into the sunset?

His gut instinct told him otherwise. Even though Dylan was convinced that his wife was gone, Jesse worried that she might still be in danger.

When he stepped outside, Nate was coming toward him, fists clenched and angry as a wet badger. He called out, "Hey! Looking for something?"

Jesse said nothing. He didn't feel the need to apologize or explain.

"If you find that ransom," Nate growled, "you'd best remember that it's on my property. That makes it mine. Possession is nine-tenths of the law."

"I assume you've already searched all these outbuildings."

"You bet I have. But if you want to poke around, go right ahead."

"When the SOF rented your property, did you provide furnishings? Like the beds?"

"My pappy bought those metal frames a long

time ago when we had a full crew, and I've never seen a need to replace them. Good, sturdy frames."

"Are any of the beds missing?"

His thin shoulders stiffened. "What the hell are you saying? Did somebody steal one of my beds?"

Jesse wasn't about to tell him about the hiding place at Fiona's house. Sharing information could only lead to trouble. "Let's head back to the horse barn."

"Fine with me." He lurched forward. His earlier swagger was gone, replaced by tension. "Maybe you can convince my ex-wife that it's okay for my son to get up on horseback. All I want to do is put him in front of me on the saddle and pace around the corral. No harm in that."

"No harm at all."

"She's turning my boy into a scaredy-cat."

He suspected that Belinda's hesitation had less to do with Mickey's safety and more about his father's demeanor. Nate's bitterness was toxic and pervasive. And mostly aimed at his neighbors, the Carlisles. "How did your feud with the Carlisles get started?"

"You really want to know?"

"That's why I asked."

"I'll tell you." Nate came to a halt, stared at the dirt beneath his boots. "Sterling Carlisle killed my pappy."

Though surprised by this allegation, Jesse kept his reaction to himself. He merely nodded.

"Happened six years ago." Nate's lips barely moved when he talked. "The sheriff called it an accident, but I know better."

"How did he die?"

"We only had about fifty head of cattle. They were in the feeding pen, getting fat before slaughter. Pappy collapsed inside the pen. He got trampled."

An ironic death for a man who swore by the procedure of confining cattle in tight pens and force-feeding. "Where does Sterling Carlisle come in?"

Nate squinted as if looking back at the past. "I heard Pappy talking to him. Arguing, real loud. Telling him that his organic methods were a bunch of baloney. He was right."

"Yeah?"

"Beef cattle don't need to roam frcc and cat grass. They're meat. Nothing but damn meat."

"Did you see anything?"

"Hell, no. I had my chores. After Mama died, I took care of the cooking and housework. It was only Pappy and me at the ranch."

Though Jesse guessed that Nate was in his mid-thirties, he sounded like a kid. Under his pappy's thumb, he hadn't fully matured. "Did you hear Sterling Carlisle make a threat?"

"Not exactly. I didn't have time to stop and eavesdrop." He jabbed the air with a gnarled finger, making his point with an invisible jury. "But I know what happened. Sterling came over here and provoked my pappy into a heart attack. Then he left without summoning help. Left him to die."

Jesse made no comment, offered no judgment. He could tell that Nate believed this unlikely scenario. His eyes shone with a fanatical fervor. His breathing was shallow and strained as if hate had squeezed the air from his lungs.

Jesse's grandfather would have said that Nate was like a man bitten by a rattler. Either the venom would work through his system or he would die a poisonous death.

Nate continued. "The Carlisles ruined us. They're so righteous. So rich. They can all go straight to hell."

Jesse wondered if Nicole was included in his hatred. She hadn't been around six years ago when his father died. "The Carlisles are suffering now. With the kidnapping."

"Nicole isn't kidnapped anymore." But a cruel smirk twisted his mouth. "The way I heard it, she told Dylan she wanted a divorce and wasn't ever coming back to him."

"You believe that? You believe she ran off with Pete Richter?"

"I never would have thought it. Richter isn't a handsome man. Handy with an ax, though. He was a logger up in Oregon."

Jesse doubted that lumberjack skills would be enough to cause Nicole to leave her husband. "What else can you tell me about Richter?"

"He didn't strike me as somebody who was going to be a cowboy for the rest of his life. He kept talking about tropical beaches and hula skirts." Nate scoffed. "Butch Thurgood is a different story. Tall and good-looking. A regular ladies' man. Nicole might have been taken with him."

But Butch was dead.

As Jesse watched Nate stalk toward the horse barn, he wished that he had more training as an interrogator. His gut instincts told him that Nate was withholding vital information, but he didn't have the key to make him open up. Nor the authority to compel him to answer questions.

Inside the horse barn, Mickey ran to his father. "Mommy says I can ride on the saddle with you."

In the blink of an eye, Nate transformed from bitter to better. He'd never be Father-of-the-Year material, but his grin appeared to be sincere. Like a king, he gestured to the horses that he didn't really own. "Take your pick, son."

Nate hadn't thought to include Abby, and the disappointment written on her face was tragic. Jesse could see Fiona holding back, trying not to be rude and demanding. She was a strange and intriguing mixture of passionate emotion and strict politeness.

Jesse was far more simple. "Nate, you forgot about Abby. We'll saddle up two horses, and I'll give her a ride, too."

"Fine with me."

Fiona beamed as if he'd done something incredibly heroic, then leaned down to her daughter's level. "What do you say, Abby?"

"Thank you, Mr. Miller."

"Sure thing, kid. Pick your horse."

Unlike Mickey, Abby knew exactly what she wanted. She marched up to the stall and pointed to a black mare with a calm manner and intelligent eyes. "I like her."

"You've got good taste," Nate said. "She's one of the best riding mounts. But she threw a shoe the other day, and I want to let her rest."

If the choice had been up to Jesse, he'd pick one of the two Arabians—beautiful, proud animals. But he was sure that Nate didn't want to use such prized horseflesh to train kids for riding. He directed Abby toward a dappled mare.

"I'll call her Chip," Abby said, "because she looks like chocolate chip ice cream."

"She probably already has a name," Fiona said.

"It's Chip," Abby insisted.

"That's a take-charge attitude," Jesse said.

"You need that when you're riding. The horse needs to know who's boss."

"Don't we all?" Fiona murmured softly. "Did you find anything?"

"Not much."

As he bridled and saddled the newly christened Chip, Jesse regretted the time he'd wasted with this trip to the Circle M. Finding the metal bed frame might confirm that someone from the Circle M—either Richter or Butch—had constructed the secret room under Fiona's barn. But that wasn't earth-shaking news.

When he lifted the saddle, his injured shoulder ached, and he was glad to step back and let Fiona take over. From the way she handled the gear, he could tell that she knew about horses.

"Like mother, like daughter," he said. "Abby must have gotten her love of ponies from you."

"I'm nowhere near as devoted," she replied with an open smile. "Before we started coming up here, I'd never been interested in horses."

"California girl," he said, remembering.

"Hurry up," Abby demanded.

Fiona rested her palm on Chip's flank. "We're ready."

"Mount up," Jesse said. "You ride. I'll lift Abby up to you."

That hadn't been the plan sanctioned by Nate Miller, but Jesse didn't see a problem. As soon as Fiona and Abby were settled on horseback, he took the bridle and led the horse into the corral.

Nate followed with Mickey, who was making wild whoops and waving his arms. Not so for Abby. She took her time on horseback seriously, paying careful attention to everything her mother said.

Belinda stepped up beside him, her fists jammed into the pockets of her black slacks. Her eyes, half hidden by shaggy brown bangs, looked worried. "Do you think Nate will be able to keep these horses?"

He shrugged. "Don't know."

"He thinks he's come into a windfall. He plans to sell his little house in town, move back here and turn this place into a horse farm." She shook her head. "I have a nasty feeling that my alimony checks are about to stop coming."

As Mickey rode by, he waved with both hands. "Look at me, Mommy. I'm riding."

"I see." She waved back.

Jesse watched Fiona and Abby. They looked good on horseback. Fiona's long brown hair in the loose ponytail tousled in the breeze as she urged Chip into a trot, then slowed to a walk, then reined to a stop. The mare responded to her directions. It had been Butch Thurgood's job to train these animals, and he'd done his job well.

"It takes work to run a horse ranch," Jesse said.

"And money." Belinda leaned her shapely hip against the corral fence. "I know Nate means well, but I worry about having Mickey visit him unsupervised. A ranch like the Circle M can be a dangerous place if you don't keep a careful eye on a child."

"It's not the ranch you're worried about."

"You're right," she said. "It's Nate. There are times when he's so angry I think his eyes are going to pop right out of his head. And he doesn't understand that Mickey's a little boy who cries when he falls down and doesn't always pay attention."

"But he cares about his son."

"His one saving grace," she conceded. "I'm not sure how Nate is going to react when I get married again."

In his opinion, she was right to be concerned. Nate had a great capacity for hate. At any given moment, he could erupt. "Is he abusive?"

"He never hit me. Or Mickey." Belinda waved to her son, who was wriggling on the saddle, impatient with his father's instructions. "But he made me feel like dirt."

Verbal abuse could be more painful than physical wounds. Belinda was a strong-looking woman with broad shoulders, but she seemed to shrink when she looked at her ex-husband.

"Breaking up with him must have been hell," he said quietly.

"You have no idea. I had no money. If Fiona hadn't given me a job, letting me move into her vacant house as a caretaker, I wouldn't have had a place to live."

He remembered something Fiona had told him. "You took out a restraining order."

"Nate wouldn't leave me alone. He wanted Mickey. Wanted his son." She shuddered. "Thank God, that part of my life is over."

Jesse hoped she was right. That Nate wouldn't cause her any more trouble.

After they finished their ride and brought the horses back into the barn, Fiona got a call on her cell. Her exhilaration about her ride with Abby dissipated as she talked.

When she disconnected, she came to him. "That was the sheriff. I need to get back to the house. Right away."

Chapter Thirteen

Fiona slammed the door to her station wagon and stormed toward her front porch. She'd arranged for Abby to go home with Belinda and Mickey because she didn't want her daughter to see what was about to happen.

Clinton had called the sheriff, demanding that he be allowed to search her house for his precious belongings. Both of them stood waiting for her. If Burke hadn't been at her house, they probably would have broken a window and entered on their own authority.

As she approached, she couldn't decide which of the two men was more hateful. Sheriff Trainer with his unfounded suspicions? Or her stepson with his unfounded demands?

Jesse strode past her, inserting himself as mediator. "Good afternoon, gentlemen. What the hell do you want?"

Clinton straightened the lapel on his tailored Harris tweed jacket and stuck his nose in the air. "We have a warrant to search this house for stolen property."

"Stolen?" She choked on the word. "In what twisted universe would you think I stole anything from you?"

"My father's property," he said smugly, "belongs to me and my sister."

"Do you think your father would be proud, Clinton?" If she'd had Jesse's gun in her hand, she wouldn't have hesitated to drill a neat little hole in the middle of his handsome forehead. "Do you think he'd applaud your greed?"

"You're stalling," he said. "Like when you accused me of breaking into your house."

"I'm not so sure you didn't."

"Don't push me, Fiona."

When Clinton took a threatening step toward her, she noticed that Agent Burke made a corresponding move. If this confrontation turned physical, she knew that Burke and Jesse would be on her side. A reassuring thought.

But this wasn't their battle, and she refused to hide behind them. The time had come for her to fight. Not for the objects Clinton had listed on his inventory but for her reputation. "I'm not a thief."

Clinton scoffed.

Jesse slipped his arm out of the sling and flexed his fingers into a fist in a not-so-subtle threat. "I suggest you show some respect to the widow."

"Settle down," the sheriff said. "We're here with a legal warrant."

"Show it to me," she said.

The sheriff placed the faxed warrant in her

hand. Attached was Clinton's inventory. Blinded by anger, she needed a moment for her eyes to focus. "It's signed by a Denver judge. Does he have jurisdiction in this district?"

"That's a valid question," Jesse said. "I'm sure Special Agent Burke can clear this up with a couple of phone calls to his bosses in the FBI. What is it that you're looking to seize? A Tiffany lamp?"

"And a pink tiara," she said, glancing at Clinton's list.

"A tiara, huh?" Jesse shot a glare in the direction of the sheriff. "That sounds like a threat to national security. Maybe we should call the NSA."

Burke juggled his cell phone. "I can start with the state attorney's office. Or the governor. He's a personal friend of Carolyn's."

"I'm just doing my job," Sheriff Trainer muttered.

He looked so cowed and miserable that Fiona

might have felt sorry for him if he hadn't been so hostile toward her. She stated, "I want this issue settled. Immediately. We have much more important things to worry about than Clinton's petty claims."

"Like what?" Clinton said.

She focused on the sheriff. "Making sure Nicole is all right. Finding the missing ransom."

"Not my problem," Clinton said. "I'm not backing down."

"I wouldn't expect you to." Her anger solidified into a hard mass in her chest, blocking her lungs. She had to speak her piece or explode. "Ever since your father died, you and your mother have made your demands exceedingly clear. With the help of your lawyers, you grabbed my house, my car and my bank accounts. But you can never take my most important possession."

"What's that?"

"Memories." If all she had left was the remembrance of her years with Wyatt, their love and their happiness, she'd be a wealthy woman.

She paused to inhale a breath. Now that she'd spoken of her pathetic financial condition in front of both the sheriff and Burke, her secret would be common knowledge. Humiliating, but probably for the best. She couldn't hide the fact that she was running out of money for much longer; soon she needed to look for a job.

She handed her house keys to Burke. "Would you please accompany Clinton while he searches? I'd appreciate if he makes as little mess as possible."

"I understand," Burke said. "This won't take long."

She watched Clinton stalk toward her house. Any hope of reconciliation with that side of Wyatt's family was gone. It pained her to realize that Abby would never know many of her blood relatives.

Jesse stood close beside her, and she was glad

for his presence. She'd handled Clinton on her own, but it didn't hurt to have a strong shoulder to lean against for comfort after he was gone.

Sheriff Trainer cleared his throat. "Was all that true? You lost everything after your husband died?"

"Pretty much," she said. "I have a clear deed to this house, but that's about all."

"That explains why you moved here." He took out his cigarettes and tapped the top of the pack. "I didn't understand why a city gal like you would want to live in this cabin. Now I know the truth. You're broke."

"That's enough," Jesse said.

"I haven't even gotten started." He gestured with his unlit cigarette. "There was one thing I couldn't figure out about Fiona and her connection to the kidnapping. I didn't know why a rich woman would get involved. But you aren't rich, are you? You have a motive."

"So do you," Jesse said coldly.

"What?" His voice was a squawk.

"That million-dollar ransom is a big motivator. I've got to ask myself, how were the kidnappers always able to keep one step ahead of the investigation? They must have somebody on the inside. You?"

"That's just plain—"

"The way I figure, you've got a lot on your plate—Butch's unsolved murder, locating Nicole and finding the missing ransom. Yet you made time to personally serve Clinton Grant's warrant. It looks like you're trying to point us in the wrong direction."

"I've got no leads."

"Why not?" Jesse asked. "Richter is no genius. He must have left clues. Unless you're covering up for him."

The sheriff fired up his cigarette. "I don't have to stand here and take this."

Fiona spoke up. "Then leave. Get off my property."

Without another word, he went to his vehicle and got behind the wheel.

Her heart was beating faster as she watched him drive away. She clasped Jesse's hand. "Thanks for backing me up."

"You could have thrown that weasel off your land without my help." He gave her hand a squeeze. "You're a lot stronger than you realize."

With adrenaline surging through her veins, she felt strong and capable, felt as if she could take on the world…as long as Jesse was there to encourage her. "Those things you said to the sheriff. Did you mean them?"

"I've got no evidence that points to him, but I'm pretty good at reading people. Sheriff Trainer has a larcenous streak. I wouldn't be surprised to find out that Clinton paid him a little something to come here and enforce that warrant."

That thought hadn't occurred to her, but it made sense. "And if he took a bribe from

Clinton, he might be susceptible to a really big payoff from the kidnappers."

"Like I said, a million in cash is a big temptation."

And so was he. His gleaming white smile drew her toward him. If Clinton hadn't been nearby, she would have gone up on tiptoe and kissed the smile off Jesse's face, capturing it for herself.

Worried that she couldn't resist him, she quickly looked away. "If we can't count on the sheriff, we have to investigate on our own."

"We?"

"You said it yourself. I'm stronger than I look."

She stretched to her full height—five feet three inches of unmitigated self-confidence. She had no intention of living under a cloud of suspicion. If the sheriff thought she was guilty of working with kidnappers, others might think so, too. And Clinton had been quick to call her a thief.

There was no shame in being broke, but she wouldn't stand for attacks on her character. She was a good person. If it meant tracking down a kidnapper to prove her integrity, she stood ready for the challenge.

Jesse was a professional bodyguard, and he knew his business. When the people who hired him wanted to carry their own weapon or show him how they knew enough karate to defeat an attacker, trouble ensued. The client got arrogant and took risks.

As he stood beside Fiona, waiting for Burke and Clinton to emerge from her house, he launched into his standard lecture to clients regarding their safety.

"The reason I'm here," he said, "is to protect you."

"And I appreciate that more than you know."

Her soft gray eyes reminded him of the skies before dawn when the light thinned and the world paused in restful silence before the new day. Though he acknowledged her inner strength, she was gentleness personified. An artist. A doting mother.

"I don't want you to be physically involved in investigating," he said. "Your job is to stay safe."

"But I've already been helping you," she said. "We searched my property together."

Apparently, she hadn't noticed his precautions. He'd been armed and alert. Wentworth had been within shouting distance. If he had sensed a threat, he would have stepped forward.

Or would he? Remembering the moment when they entered the barn, he'd been apprehensive. The shadows in that old structure seemed to have form and menace. Instinctively, his hand had gone to his gun. But he hadn't turned back, hadn't returned her to the safety of her house.

A serious lapse in judgment. It worried him. While focusing on the investigation, he hadn't been an efficient bodyguard. That had to change. Though they hadn't yet encountered a direct threat to Fiona's safety, Richter was still at large. Still dangerous.

Burke held open the door to her house, and Clinton marched through, scowling and imperious at the same time. Jesse guessed that he hadn't found what he was looking for.

"No tiara," Burke announced gleefully. "We didn't find a single item on the inventory list."

"Because I don't have them," Fiona said clearly.

A more honorable man than Clinton would have offered an apology. He gave a sniff and looked away. "My business here is concluded."

"Fine with me," she said. "If I *never* see you again, I'll have no regrets. But don't forget Abby, your half sister. She deserves a chance to know her family."

Unsmiling, he said, "I suppose."

"You and your sister are welcome to see her. Any time."

"Maybe," he said grudgingly. "Someday."

As Clinton drove away, Jesse looked up to the

sky. There were only a few hours of daylight left. Time seemed to be slipping through his fingers. Today's investigation had filled in a few blanks, but they hadn't made much forward progress.

Jesse wasn't playing to his strengths. He didn't have the logical skills of a detective or the glib cleverness of an interrogator. He was a hunter. If hc hoped to find the ransom and learn what had really happened to Nicole, he needed to trust his instincts.

Fiona looked at him expectantly. "What do we do next?"

There was that word again. *We.* "I want you to hook up with Wentworth at the Carlisle place. He'll drive you into town to pick up Abby. Then back here."

"I don't want to hide," she said. "I need to be involved. There must be something I can do. Some way I can help with the investigation."

Everything about her—from the glow in her eyes to the way her expressive hands held out a plea—was an invitation. Dealing with Clinton brought out the feistiness in her; she was ready for action.

"You don't have any experience in hunting," he said.

"None."

"And you can't handle a firearm."

"But I'm a really good observer," she said. "I have an artist's eye for detail."

"That's one point in your favor."

"And I'm good at following orders. I'll do whatever you tell me. Except for stay home."

He frankly thought the risk was minimal. And he didn't want to disappoint her. He turned to Burke. "We're going to need two horses."

Chapter Fourteen

Jesse preferred hunting alone. When he was a boy, his grandfather showed him the value of quiet observation. He learned when to wait and how to pursue his quarry, not only by following the tracks but also by listening and sensing. It was his nature to hunt. He never killed for sport, only for food. His grandfather taught him to respect all living things—the wapiti, the hare, the quail—that provided nourishment.

This hunting expedition was different. His

prey was a criminal, who he held in low regard. And he was most definitely not alone.

According to Burke's notes, the ransom was delivered at the same time the FBI operation was under way and while Dylan was meeting with his wife for the last time.

The ransom was delivered by Carolyn to a field west of the Carlisle ranch house. That would be their starting place. He and Fiona rode with Burke and Carolyn. As was her habit, Carolyn took the lead.

The terrain beyond the Carlisle ranch house spread from a vast, open valley covered with dry winter grasses and sagebrush to forested foothills. As the sun dipped lower, the shadows grew longer.

He rode close to Fiona. Her long brown hair streamed down her back under her fawn-colored cowboy hat. Though small and wiry, she handled her gray horse with skill. In spite of her sneakers, the former California girl looked as though she belonged in the saddle.

They slowed as they approached the barbed-wire fence surrounding a pasture. She gazed toward him with sparkling eyes. "Thanks for letting me come."

He liked having her here. Wherever she went, Fiona had a calming effect. "I want you to use your powers of observation. Your artist's eye might notice a detail that escapes the rest of us."

Her eyes narrowed as she scanned the surrounding forest. "What kind of detail?"

"What do you see?"

"The big picture," she said. "Vast and wide open. Faraway peaks covered with snow. This landscape is spectacular but subtle as well, with a monochromatic palette ranging from sandstone pink to khaki grasses to deep, rich mahogany shadows." She breathed a reverent sigh. "I love being here."

"Wait until it snows," he warned.

"I'm looking forward to it. A white Christmas."

Carolyn stopped at the gate in the barbed-wire fence. With a flick of her reins, her horse, Elvis, wheeled around to face them. "The kidnapper told me to bring the ransom here. I had the money in one of those huge mountaineering backpacks. He told me to leave it by La Rana."

"What's that?" Fiona asked.

Carolyn pointed to a fat rock formation in the middle of the field. It resembled a giant toad. "La Rana, the frog."

Inside the barbed wire were water troughs and feeding stations. The earth had been trampled to a mix of dirt and hay.

"When she delivered the ransom," Burke said, "there were three hundred head of Black Angus in this field. We moved them to get a better look at the crime scene."

A man had been shot and killed at this site. The ranch foreman. He was a traitor, had been feeding information to the kidnappers. But his last act on this earth had been one of loyalty—trying to protect Carolyn.

Jesse dismounted, went to the gate and unlatched it. "Show me what you did, Carolyn."

She rode through the gate, swung down from Elvis and joined him. "I went through here, dodging around the cattle."

Fiona followed in Carolyn's footsteps, leaving her horse behind. "That must have been terrifying. Those cattle are huge."

"Over a thousand pounds each. This field is the last stop before the slaughterhouse, so these cattle were fully grown."

"She wasn't scared," Burke said. "Carolyn loves her cows."

"They're beautiful creatures," she said. "But when the gunfire started and the herd got spooked, I was plenty worried."

"How did you get out of here alive?"

"Burke." She glanced over her shoulder and

gave him a grin. "He rode in here and saved me. My hero."

"Aw, shucks," he said. "Any decent cowboy would have done the same."

Carolyn laughed. "As if you're a cowboy? What kind of cowboy wears a Cubs cap?"

"A cowboy from Chicago."

Jesse strode across the dirt toward the boulder, La Rana. "Where was the kidnapper?"

"I never actually saw him. But he was near the rocks. That's where the gunshots came from. And the ransom was gone almost as quickly as I left it."

Burke, still on horseback, rode up beside him. "We tried to gather evidence, but there was nothing. The cattle obliterated everything. Didn't even find a footprint."

The kidnapper had come up with a simple and effective plan for grabbing the money. He lured Carolyn into the pen, fired his weapon and spooked the cattle. She was too busy trying to make it to the fence to go after him. "How fast did Burke get here?"

"Five to ten minutes."

"In the confusion," Burke said, "the kidnapper made his getaway."

Jesse leaned his back against the rocks and surveyed the area. Hundreds of cattle and dozens of horses trod this patch of earth. Picking out the track of the kidnapper inside the enclosure would be impossible.

Beyond the fence, a couple of dirt truck paths crossed back and forth, providing access for delivering feed to the pasture. The forest reached almost to the edge of the fence on the north side of the barbed wire.

If Jesse had been planning a getaway, he would have preferred the mobility of being on horseback to using a vehicle. "Did you see his horse?"

"Afraid not," Carolyn said. "I was dancing as fast as I could, trying not to get squashed."

Jesse returned to his horse, stuck his boot into

the stirrup and braced himself for the jab of pain that came from using his shoulder. The stress on his body was taking a toll, but he couldn't take the time to sit back and recuperate. The fastest route to full recovery would be to find the ransom.

"Where are we going?" Fiona asked.

"We'll search along the perimeter of the barbed wire on the north side," he said. "The kidnapper had to get out of this enclosure, carrying a ransom. His horse must have been tethered in the trees."

"We already searched," Burke said. "None of the fencing was cut."

Still, there might be a sign where the kidnapper slipped through. They left the enclosure and rode slowly along the fence line. Five horizontal strands of barbed wire stretched from weathered posts. The lower two feet were reinforced with chicken wire that would act as a break against snowdrifts.

Jesse knew from experience that climbing through a barbed wire fence was a lot harder than it looked. All it took was one snag to get hopelessly entangled. But these fences weren't impermeable.

Hoofprints at the edge of the fence showed the efforts of a search team, and also obscured any prints from the kidnapper. He wished he could have searched immediately after the ransom had been delivered. The ground was too dry and hard to take neat, perfect footprints. But there would have been broken twigs and shrubs.

He swung his horse around and started back again. "Who were your searchers, Burke?"

"The FBI team had their hands full, rounding up the survivalist gun smugglers. As soon as they were free, we sent the chopper over this area with a spotlight."

That method was akin to using a monkey wrench when you needed a pair of tweezers. Tracking was about noticing the tiny details.

"And the sheriff," Burke said. "He and his deputies looked over here."

"Sheriff Trainer seems to be establishing a regular pattern of searching and not finding."

He paused at a spot where the top strand of wire had been pulled loose from the staple attaching it to the post. In the packed earth outside the fence, he saw rectangular marks about eighteen inches apart.

"Over here." He pointed to the sharp-edged tracks in the dried grass about ten feet away from the fence.

Carolyn dismounted and measured the distance between the two marks with her hands. "A ladder. He rested a ladder on the top wire and climbed over."

"Consistent with his m.o.," Burke said. "Low-tech."

"But effective," Carolyn said. "No wonder he got out of here so fast."

Burke scowled. "How did we miss this?"

"Good question," Jesse said. Once again, he was thinking of Sheriff Trainer. He'd been quick to point the finger of suspicion at Fiona. To divert it from himself?

"I don't get it," Fiona said. "Did the kidnapper make a getaway on horseback while he was carrying the backpack with the ransom and a ladder, too?"

"He must have disposed of the ladder." Jesse peered into the thick forest. "If they'd made a full search with one man posted every three feet, they would have found it."

"And what would that prove?" she asked.

"Not a damn thing. We don't need the ladder. Finding this track is enough."

"Enough for what?" She cocked her head, curious about his process. "We already know the kidnapper was here and took the ransom. So what are we looking for?"

"We want to pick up his trail, which probably starts somewhere in those trees.

Then we can track him, figure out where he went from here."

She gave a quick nod. "Got it."

"Spread out," Jesse said. "Let's move into the trees."

They dismounted and led their horses into the forest. Daylight was fading, and he hoped they could pick up the trail before dusk settled. Tracking at night presented a whole other set of problems.

It was Fiona who called out, "I found something."

He hadn't expected her to be able to notice a track. She wasn't a hunter. "What is it?"

"Well, I stepped in it. There was a horse here, and he left behind a nasty little present." She stood with her foot in the air above a dried pile of manure. "Can I wipe off my sneaker?"

"No way." Jesse turned to Burke. "Those road apples are evidence, right?"

He stifled a chuckle. "Absolutely."

Jesse took out his cell phone. "Stand right there, Fiona. I need a photo of this. Lift that foot up a little higher."

Aware that she was being teased, she pointed her toe and posed. "How's this?"

He took the shot. Even with dried manure on her shoe, she was damned cute. "Okay, now let's zoom in for a close-up."

"I'll zoom you." Laughing, she dragged the sole of her shoe across the trunk of a tree. "Okay, smart guy. I found where the horse was. Let's see you do your tracking thing."

His "tracking thing" turned out to be easier than he expected. He hunkered down and studied the hoof marks. Immediately, he noticed, "This horse was missing a right front shoe."

"Like the horse at the Circle M," Fiona said.

"The black mare that Abby wanted to ride." That minor irregularity meant this track would stand out from the many others. "Finally. We caught a break."

244 Bodyguard Under the Mistletoe

"What break?" Carolyn demanded. "What are you two talking about?"

Fiona explained, "We were over at the Circle M earlier today. One of the horses owned by the SOF had thrown a shoe. The kidnapper must have been riding that horse when he picked up the ransom."

"Which means," Jesse said, "that we now have a trail."

His instincts were leading them in the right direction. Though he wasn't a detective, he had found the key to this investigation by being true to himself. He should have done that from the start, followed the course of less thinking and more action.

THOUGH FIONA WOULD have enjoyed staying with Jesse and Burke while they tracked, the trail got really complicated: uphill into the forest, then across a rocky area and down to a dirt path. It was obvious that they'd be tracking for hours, and she needed to pick up her daughter from Belinda's.

She and Carolyn returned to the Carlisle ranch house.

Inside, they were greeted by Carolyn's mother, Andrea. A tall, slim woman in denim and cashmere, Andrea greeted them with a warm smile. She didn't hug. Andrea was reserved.

She'd divorced Sterling Carlisle and left the ranch when Carolyn and Dylan were children. Fiona couldn't imagine ever leaving Abby, no matter what the circumstance. But she was sympathetic to Andrea, who—according to Carolyn—had wanted the children to move with her to New York City. Both Carolyn and Dylan had chosen the ranch.

As an adult, Carolyn had spent some time with her mother, who was remarried and had a twelve-year-old daughter. Their relationship seemed okay. When Carolyn called her mother and told her that Nicole had been kidnapped,

Andrea hopped on a plane and came to the ranch to offer her support in this time of family crisis.

Dylan hadn't been happy to see his mother.

"Good news," Carolyn told her. "We found a track from the kidnapper's horse. Burke and Jesse are following the trail."

A frown pinched Andrea's brow. "I wish there was more I could do. I feel so helpless."

"We all do," Fiona said.

"You must stay for dinner," Andrea said to her. "You and your adorable daughter."

"It's been a long day," she said. "Especially for Abby. I think it's best if I take her home and get her to bed early."

Until that moment, she hadn't realized how anxious she was to get home. She was looking forward to tonight when she would spend time alone with Jesse. He'd promised to return to her house after he and Burke reached the end of their trail.

She had a fleeting thought of sitting close beside him on the sofa, their thighs touching. He'd caress her cheek. She'd trace the line of that tiny scar on his chin. She dragged herself out of her reverie. "But thank you, Andrea."

"Maybe tomorrow I could come to your house for a visit," she said. "Carolyn tells me that you're an artist. I'd like to see your work."

Fiona sensed something more than polite interest in her comment. "I don't have many pieces here. I left several sculptures in storage with an artist friend in Denver, and there's a shop in Cherry Creek that takes my pottery on consignment."

"You might want to dig out your portfolio," Carolyn said as she patted her mother on the shoulder. "Mom runs an art gallery in Manhattan."

With another smile, Andrea said, "I'm always looking for new talent."

Fiona blinked as if a flashbulb had exploded

in her face. Opportunities appeared in mysterious ways. "A gallery?"

"I try to showcase artists from across the country. What's your focus?"

"Right now I'm working on pottery that's a variation on the Navajo wedding vase with a drinking spout on each side."

"I'd love to see it," Andrea said. "Tomorrow morning?"

"It's a date."

This timing couldn't be better. She'd been working on a Web site to sell her handiwork. If Fiona could get her worked placed in a Manhattan gallery, her reputation would increase by leaps and bounds. It might even be possible for her to make a living selling her art.

As she hurried out the door with Wentworth, a shiver went through her. Earlier today, her outlook had been pretty gloomy. But now things seemed to be going well. *Maybe too well.*

For one thing, Jesse and Burke had found a tangible trail that might lead to the ransom.

For another, Carolyn's mother had opened the door to possible career opportunity.

And then, there was Jesse. The attraction she felt toward him was growing deeper with every shared glance, every smile, every laugh. An electricity arced between them whenever they touched. She couldn't deny that their friendship was poised on the verge of becoming something more. And wouldn't that be…amazing? To make love again? To spend the night in his sheltering embrace? It was too much to hope for.

Another shiver creased her spine. Being too happy was dangerous.

Chapter Fifteen

The kidnapper had taken an erratic escape route, dodging into the cover of the trees, up toward a ridge, down to the fence, then back to the forest. Jesse read the tracks and the mind-set of the man who made them—a man who was running scared.

At the time of the ransom pickup, all hell had been breaking loose. Burke described three hundred cattle in the pen, bawling and jostling. A dozen ranch hands poured into the area near La Rana. Two other FBI operations were under way. There had been helicopters, bullhorns and armed assault teams.

No wonder the kidnapper had been clashing back and forth. He was a villain and a criminal but also a mouse peeking out of his hole and hoping to get away.

Finally, he'd settled on a route, eventually leaving the Carlisle Ranch and riding parallel to the main road. Since his horse had lost a shoe, he avoided the hard surface of the pavement. *A lucky break for Jesse.* He had a trail to follow, and it led into Riverton.

By the time he and Burke reached the edge of town, dusk had turned to darkness.

Jesse dismounted and shone his flashlight on a hoofprint at the shoulder of the road. There was no corresponding print on the opposite side. He walked to the corner of the street and back again, finding plenty of other footprints and the track of a mountain bike. No hoofprints. "This is it. End of the trail."

He surveyed the area. There were mailboxes on posts and long driveways. Lights shone through the windows of small frame houses, set back from the road. A single streetlight cast dim illumination on the rural neighborhood.

"There could be witnesses," Burke said.

"In a town like Riverton, seeing a man on horseback wouldn't be unusual."

"You never know. I'll contact the sheriff and have his men canvass the area."

"Sheriff Trainer." Jesse spoke the name with undisguised disgust. "He's already missed too many clues. His men should have found these tracks."

"Doubtful." Burke adjusted his baseball cap. "I've done my fair share of hunting, and I've never seen anybody follow a trail the way you just did, especially in the dark. Admit it, Jesse. You're half bloodhound."

Jesse grinned. "Are you calling me a dog?"

"Where the hell did you learn how to track like this?"

"When I was a kid, I spent summers on the reservation with my grandfather, a wise man. He taught me a lot."

"Ute?"

"Navajo." Jesse turned toward the lights of the main street in town. He hated to think they'd come this far to reach a dead end. "Why was he headed into town?"

"He must have planned to meet up with his buddy," Burke said. "I can't think of anybody else he'd want to see in Riverton. Most of the townsfolk thought the Sons of Freedom were troublemakers."

"The track we've been following," Jesse said, "do you think it was Butch or Richter?"

"My gut tells me it was Richter. When the ransom was being delivered, he was quick on the trigger. Just like he was when he shot you."

"My gut agrees with yours." Obviously, Richter was the more dangerous of the two. "But if Richter had the ransom, why did he kill his partner?"

254   *Bodyguard Under the Mistletoe*

"Greed." One of the most common and deadly of motives.

"Carrying a million dollars in a backpack, he sure as hell wouldn't want to be seen. There had to be a damn good reason why he risked coming into town. More than that, why did he cross the road here? At this particular street?"

Burke concluded, "His destination in Riverton—wherever it was—must be nearby."

A block away was the main commercial strip. They mounted and rode at a walk on the edge of the pavement toward the stop sign. Riverton was too small to merit a stoplight or a grocery store. The people who lived here shopped in Delta where Jesse had been in the hospital.

Though it was only seven o'clock, most of the storefronts were dark, except for their twinkling Christmas decorations. The only activity seemed to be at the far end of the block-long business district where the tavern and the diner were located. A number of cars and trucks were parked at the curb outside those two establishments.

They approached the gas station, a shabby-looking place. The office windows were streaked with grime, as were the three garage doors on the repair bays.

"I've never seen this gas station open," Burke said. "The old guy who runs it keeps his own schedule."

"Silas O'Toole." Jesse remembered the incident that took place when he and Wentworth had driven through town. "I saw him in action with a double-barrel shotgun in his hands, warning some cowboy to get off his property."

"What was the argument about? A flat tire?"

"O'Toole has a grandson who works with him. A mechanic, I guess. Silas mentioned his parole officer. The grandson took off before he had finished some work for the cowboy."

"He left town," Burke said. "When?"

"Right after I got out of the hospital. The day

after the ransom was delivered." Jesse paused. The significance of this episode was beginning to sink in. "Damn it, I should have paid more attention."

The timing was right. O'Toole's grandson could have been working with Richter and Butch, could have gotten a payoff from them and blown town. *Why didn't I make this connection sooner?* There wasn't time for mistakes.

Jesse dismounted. His boots hit the pavement of the parking lot outside the gas station and jolted him into a state of alertness. There was one light over the pumps and one over the door. He needed his flashlight to peer into corners.

Around the back of the station, four cars—all in varying states of disrepair—were parked. The stink of oil, gas and grit hung in the air. He and Burke prowled, looking for hoofprints in the mud. He needed a sign, an indication that the kidnapper had been here.

"I should have paid more attention," he said.

"A grizzled old guy in overalls waving a shotgun is a pretty big clue."

"Or just local color," Burke muttered. "I'll tell you what. I've had enough of ranches and cattle and cowboys. Can't wait to get back to my office in Denver."

"What about Carolyn?"

"She works in Denver, too. Don't let her cowgirl persona fool you. She's a high-powered businesswoman who likes sushi for lunch and Gucci for shoes. It's a damn good thing. I love Carolyn, but I don't think I could live out here."

"I could."

Though he hadn't been thinking about settling down here, or anywhere else for that matter, Jesse enjoyed mountain living. Every view was as pretty as a postcard. The air was fresh. He liked being here, especially because Fiona was here.

The minute he thought of her, his heart beat

a little faster. A vision of her gentle smile filled his mind. He saw her long hair flowing behind her as she rode beside him. Tonight, they'd have some quiet time together. He'd make sure of that.

At the front of the gas station, he twisted the handle on the door to the office, hoping that O'Toole's lax business practices extended to leaving the place wide open. No such luck. The door was locked.

He went to the repair bays and yanked on the first garage door. Also locked.

The second door slid up with a loud screech that made their horses jump. He turned to Burke and grinned. "Ready for a little breaking and entering?"

"No problem. I'm an FBI special agent."

"Which doesn't put you above the law."

"But gives me a lot of experience in coming up with plausible, semilegal excuses."

Jesse entered the garage and turned on the

bare-bulb lights. The inside of the auto repair area gave new meaning to the concept of neglect. Tools scattered across a grime-encrusted counter. Grease-stained rags overflowed a metal barrel. A worn calendar from 2002 showed a sexy redhead in black leather chaps leaning against a motorcycle. These concrete floors didn't look as though they'd been swept since the day that calendar was new.

It didn't take long to find a hoofprint on the floor, clearly outlined in a combination of mud and grease. "There was a horse in here, but this hoof has a shoe. There's no way of knowing if it was the kidnapper's mount."

"It was him." Burke rose from the floor where he'd been picking through a pile of trash. "I might not be a bloodhound, but when it comes to finding money, I'm top dog."

In his gloved hand, he held a grease-stained one-hundred-dollar bill. Part of the ransom.

AFTER FIONA GOT ABBY to bed and made sure Wentworth was comfortable, she got busy in her studio at the rear of the house. Tomorrow, Carolyn's mother would be coming to see her work, and Fiona wanted to show her best pieces.

She still needed to finish the glaze on her interpretation of a Navajo wedding vase. Her intention had never been to create a replica; she didn't presume to understand the rituals of the wedding ceremony. Instead, she'd taken inspiration from the idea of two spouts rising from one vessel: one for the bride, the other for the groom. She liked the idea of both drinking from the same source while maintaining a separate identity.

Though she'd started with the traditional coiled pot method, her creation was more fanciful. The long spouts rose from delicate vines that curled around the pot with overlapping leaves—an effect that was both modern and organic.

She carefully painted a pearly white glaze on

the once-fired bisque-ware. The design was elaborate enough without painted embellishment.

Since it didn't make sense to fire up the kiln for only one piece, she found herself adding glazes to a couple of other chalices and cups. The theme of her current work seemed to be drinking. Was she thirsting for something?

"Jesse," she murmured.

These designs had been completed before she met him. But since the moment when she first recognized the man who saved her husband's life, Jesse had never been far from her mind. She'd been ready for him to come into her life.

After placing the pottery in the kiln, she carefully put away the glazing chemicals that she kept in a locked cabinet far out of Abby's reach. She set the timer on the kiln.

What else could she show to Andrea? She pulled open the cabinet doors and started opening boxes that she hadn't touched since she moved into the cabin. Going through these pots and sculptures was like reading a diary.

Before Abby was born, her work had been bigger. The largest piece was two feet tall—an eruption of roses that she'd saved because the coppery glaze was so vivid. She'd been thinking of her marriage when she sculpted this bouquet. Though it was bright and happy, the technique lacked maturity and depth.

After her daughter was born and her time for work was more limited, she made several whimsical little houses. Dwellings for fairies. Her plan had been to build an elfin city, a magical place. Many of these houses had sold, but she still had a few left.

After her husband's death, her work turned predictably dark. Charred vases. Jagged abstract shapes. She opened a box and took out an eight-inch-tall sculpture. A tree struck by lightning with clawlike branches and a glaze that reflected dark, bloodred in the crevices.

The tree appeared to be screaming and dying. When she'd carved these lines, she'd been driven by sorrow and rage. Now she could turn it around in her hands and calmly admire the emotion without being affected by it. "Not bad."

Definitely, she'd show this one to Andrea.

Though her kiln was properly vented, the small studio always got extrahot when she was firing her work. She stripped down to her black sports bra.

Even if Andrea didn't want any of her work for her gallery in Manhattan, this was a useful project. She could photograph these pieces for her Web site. She dug deeper into the cabinets, looking for a photo portfolio of some pieces she had on consignment in Denver.

Andrea had asked for her focus, but Fiona hadn't really settled on a particular style. Her pottery reflected her emotional state, which ranged from happy as a cloud to miserable as a lump of coal.

She wanted to sculpt Jesse. His handsome face showed depth of character. His hands were gentle but strong. Creative energy raced through her veins. Where was her sketchbook? She hadn't felt so dynamic in a very long time.

In a burst, she sketched him. Wearing a flat-brim cowboy hat. Clenching a fist. His dark eyes were fierce. His smile was predatory and, at the same time, sexy as hell. Oh, yes, she'd like to be devoured by him.

A rivulet of sweat trickled between her breasts. Her ponytail was damp on her neck. The intense heat came partly from her kiln, but mostly from an internal fire. She needed to take a break before she erupted.

Leaving her studio, she went through the kitchen to the back door, unfastened the locks and stepped outside. The chill of the night air rippled around her. She lifted her hair off her neck.

When she inhaled a gulp of air, her lungs cooled. She exhaled a contented sigh. She'd been utterly consumed by artistic inspiration, and it felt amazing.

The world settled slowly around her, and she became aware of night rustlings. The wind rattled the bare branches of the aspens at the front of the house.

She noticed movement among the pine trees near the barn. Then she saw him clearly. A man separated from the shadows. He was moving fast, coming right at her. He had a gun in his hand.

Chapter Sixteen

At the ramshackle home of Silas O'Toole, Jesse followed while Burke took the lead. He liked the big FBI agent and thought they made good partners.

Burke was particularly adept at logistics. With a couple of phone calls, he'd found O'Toole's address and arranged for a few ranch hands to drive into town, take their horses back to the stable and provide them with an SUV.

Burke hammered on the door. "Open up. FBI."

Remembering O'Toole's double-barrel shotgun, Jesse had drawn his weapon. He held it down at his side in his right hand. His left shoulder had begun to ache. If he hadn't been running on adrenaline, he would have been tired.

"Silas O'Toole." Burke pounded on the door again. "FBI."

The frame house was midsize, set back from the street on a large front lot covered with dead weeds. An old beat-up sofa sat on the porch. A light shone through a curtained window, and Jesse could hear the television from inside.

The door creaked open. Silhouetted by the dim light inside the house was an old man with wild hair. He wore faded red long johns under baggy jeans that hung from his hips.

Silas growled, "What do you want, Mr. FBI man?"

"We're looking for Zeke O'Toole. Is your grandson here?"

"Nope."

When he started to close the door, Burke blocked it with his foot. "We need to talk."

The old man's eyes were tired. His scrawny shoulders slumped. "What the hell has Zeke done this time?"

"Can we come in?"

O'Toole stepped back. "Suit yourself."

The interior was dingy. A half-eaten sandwich and a can of beer sat on a littered coffee table in front of the television. Using the remote, O'Toole turned off the TV. He flopped into an armchair.

Jesse stood behind Burke, allowing him to ask the questions. "Do you know where Zeke is?"

"Grand Junction, most likely. A couple of days ago, he sold a car. Got cash for it. That money was burning a hole in his pocket. The boy went into Grand Junction to have himself a good time. Ain't nothing wrong with that."

"When did he sell the car?" Burke asked.

"I don't know. Maybe the day before yesterday. Zeke don't tell me everything."

"But he lives here," Burke said.

"When he's between girlfriends, he comes back here. It ain't much, but it's home."

Jesse figured that the cash payment came from the ransom. After the pickup, Richter rode into town to the gas station, where he took the car from Zeke.

As Burke questioned the old man about his grandson's friends and possible association with Richter and Butch, Jesse felt his cell phone vibrate in his pocket. He took it out. Wentworth was calling.

Turning his head, he answered, "What's up?"

"Somebody came after Fiona."

A shock jolted Jesse's system. His fingers tightened on the phone. "Is she all right?"

"She's fine." Though Wentworth's voice was steady, a note of urgency tinged his words. "I didn't see the guy. She said he was running toward her, coming from the barn. He had a gun."

"Was she outside?"

"She went out the back door. It was only for a second."

Long enough for her to be shot or abducted or scared to death. What the hell had she been thinking? He'd told her a dozen times that she wasn't to leave the house. He should have been there to protect her.

"On my way," he said. "I'll be there in less than ten minutes."

FIONA STOOD AT THE foot of her daughter's bed and watched her child sleep. The light from the hallway shone on Abby's round, cherubic face and her blond curls. So sweet. So completely innocent.

More than anything, Fiona wanted to grab Abby out of the bed and carry her away to somewhere safe. How could they possibly stay here? The armed man who came running at her through the shadows was a tangible threat—different than hearing voices in the night or assuming there might be danger.

He was real.

The instant she'd seen him, she'd dodged back into the house, called for Wentworth and locked the door. Was it Richter? The kidnapper? What did he want?

Her arms yearned to hold Abby, but she didn't want to pass her terror on to her child. It was far better if Abby stayed asleep and unaware. Facing the threat was her mother's job. Fiona's job.

Leaving the bedroom door open, she went down the hall to the front room. Her gaze fastened on the closed curtains at the window, and she shuddered. He could be out there, hiding in the shadows, peering inside. She pulled her sweater more tightly around herself.

"Jesse is on the way," Wentworth said.

"He's not going to be happy. I went outside. I broke his rules."

"He'll get over it." Wentworth leaned against the door leading into the kitchen with his gun in his hand. "Jesse never stays mad for long."

Though she shouldn't have gone out the door, her action had provoked a response. At least, she knew that her suspicions had a basis in fact. Someone was watching her.

From outside, she heard a vehicle approaching.

Wentworth moved to the window and peeked before unlocking the front door.

A car door slammed. In seconds, Jesse charged through the door. So much energy exploded around him that the air seemed to ripple. His eyes were fierce. Without breaking stride, he came toward her. His strong arms encircled her and held her close.

She clung to him for all she was worth. Her tears came quickly. Tears of relief. He was here. Her protector. She was safe. She literally trusted Jesse with her life. He'd never let anything bad happen to her or Abby.

He murmured, "Are you okay?"

"A little scared."

He stroked her hair. "Do you want to tell me why you went outside?"

"Not really." She wiped the dampness from her cheeks and looked up at him. "But I will."

"Okay."

She owed him an explanation. His instructions about staying in the house had been explicit. "I fired up the kiln in my studio. The room was really hot, and I thought I'd step out for a minute to cool off."

He glanced over his shoulder at Wentworth. "Where were you?"

"Front room, sitting on my butt and thinking everything was fine."

"It's okay. Not your fault," Jesse said.

"By the time I heard Fiona call for help," Wentworth said, "she was already back inside and locking the door. We both went down the hall to Abby's bedroom."

With his arm still around her, Jesse escorted her to the sofa in the front room. After he seated her, he spoke to Wentworth. "Agent Burke and two other ranch hands are waiting outside. I'll stay with Fiona. You take charge. See if you can find this creep."

"And be careful," she piped up. "He has a gun."

The door closed behind Wentworth, and Jesse sat close beside her. She snuggled under his arm and rested her head on his chest. His jacket still held the cold from the night, but his body heat warmed his shirt. For a long moment, she listened to the steady beating of his heart.

"Jesse, what am I going to do? I can't stay here. Not with some crazy person running around."

"You're worried about Abby," he said.

"Tell me what to do." She looked up into the depths of his dark eyes. "I trust you."

Though they were nestled together, his kiss surprised her. This wasn't a gentle, reassuring kiss. It was hard and demanding. Hot.

Unaware of her movements, she shifted position on the sofa until she was facing him. Her body pressed hard against his chest. There were too damn many clothes in the way. She wanted to be part of him, wanted him to make love to her.

His tongue forced her lips apart, and she welcomed him into her mouth. He exhaled a groan and the sound excited her even more.

When they broke apart, she was breathless and eager for more. She ducked her head and dove toward him, seeking another intense kiss.

"Wait," he said.

"Why?"

"Think about it," he said.

She'd been through a long dry spell when it came to sex, and she was thirsty, parched. She licked her lips.

Of course, they couldn't make love right now. The timing was all wrong. Burke and Wentworth were outside but could return at any moment. Abby was sleeping down the hall. And a madman had threatened her with a gun.

"All right," she said. "Not right now. But soon."

"I never should have left you here alone."

"You didn't. Wentworth was here." She caressed the plane of his cheek. "You've done everything right."

He lifted her off his lap, returning her to a position beside him on the sofa cushions. "I'm glad you trust me."

"Why wouldn't I? Longbridge Security is the best in the West."

"My reputation is no guarantee. You saw what happened to Nicole."

With a quick peck on her forehead, he rose from the sofa and went toward the kitchen. She followed behind him. "You know how I feel about guilt. There's no point to it. You can't blame yourself for what's happening to Nicole. My God, you almost died trying to rescue her."

He opened her refrigerator door and took out

a bottled water. "I'm mad. At myself. I failed to protect my client."

And she knew that he wouldn't rest until he found the ransom and Nicole. "Where did the trail lead?"

"To another suspect. Nothing definite."

He took a long taste of the water, and she watched his Adam's apple bob up and down. He'd been on horseback for hours and had to be exhausted. Only a few days ago, he'd been in a coma and near death. "Are you in pain?"

"Hey, I'm the one worrying about you. Trying to figure out what we should do to keep you safe."

"I could pack up and move to a motel." Though she didn't like to spend the money, she wouldn't hesitate if it meant keeping Abby safe. "I hate to tell Abby what's going on. I don't want her to have nightmares."

"I'll keep two men posted outside your house tonight, and I'll stay inside. We ought to be fine."

He reached toward her. His fingers combed through her hair. "I wish I could promise you that I'd keep you and Abby safe. Wish that I could say I've never lost a client. But it's not true. I've made mistakes."

"You saved my husband's life."

In a way, he was saving her, too. Bringing her back to life. Reminding her of what it meant to be a woman.

"Three years ago, I was hired as a body-guard for the family of the CEO of an oil company. They were vacationing at a private lodge in Telluride. I had two other men with me, expert skiers."

"Do you ski?" she asked.

"And snowboard. Why does that surprise you? I grew up in Colorado."

"So, you ski, ride, hunt and are an expert marksman. What about rock climbing and canoeing?"

He nodded. "It's part of the package for

Longbridge Security. We protect people who are active in outdoor activities."

"Is there anything you don't do?"

"I get seasick," he admitted. "I'm fine on rivers with a canoe or kayak, but put me on the open sea and I turn green and puke my guts out."

It was nice to know that he wasn't expert at everything. "Sorry for interrupting. Go ahead with your story."

Before he could continue, there was a rap on the front door. They returned to the front room, and Jesse unlocked the dead bolt to admit Wentworth, Burke and two cowboys from the Carlisle Ranch.

Burke sank down onto the sofa and groaned loudly. "I don't know how you guys ride all day. My butt is killing me."

Fiona glanced down the hall toward her daughter's bedroom. "Sorry about your butt, but would you all mind moving to the kitchen? Abby's sleeping."

280 Bodyguard Under the Mistletoe

The men tromped across the floor. Loud as a herd of Angus. Burke groaned again as he sat in a kitchen chair and stretched his long legs out in front of him.

"We didn't find him," he said. "But there were plenty of signs that somebody has been lurking around here."

"Did he leave a trail?" Jesse asked.

"After spending the day with you," Burke said, "I was able to follow his tracks. He went to the driveway, then down to the road. Then nothing."

Fiona busied herself making coffee. Her supply of healthy snacks had dwindled to a couple of packages of granola bars, which she placed on the table while Jesse outlined the bodyguard schedule for the night.

She stood by the counter, watching the coffee drip into the glass pot, trying to make sense of the situation. She looked toward the five men gathered at her table. An FBI agent. Two cowboys. Wentworth. And Jesse.

"I have a question," she said.

Their heads turned toward her. In their over-whelmingly masculine presence, she felt small and feminine. But she wasn't helpless, couldn't allow herself to be a shy little violet. The safety of her child was at stake.

"This afternoon," she said, "we were following the track of the kidnapper who picked up the ransom. Which one was it?"

"We don't know for sure," Burke said. "But we're figuring it was Richter."

"So he had the money," she reasoned.

"Then he killed his partner," Burke said.

"Why?" Her voice was louder than she intended. "He has the money. His partner is dead. Why is he still hanging around?"

"He *had* the money," Jesse said. "But he must have lost it. Butch might have gotten it away from him. Or even Nicole."

Burke added, "When the ransom was being delivered, there were dozens of FBI swarming the area. SWAT teams. Helicopters. They might have figured they should hide the cash and lie low."

"And there's a fine hiding place in your barn."

She pieced together the logic. "So, one of them brought the money here and hid it."

"It's possible," Burke said.

"Then what? The ransom just disappeared?"

No one had an answer.

Without further evidence, they were playing a guessing game. All she knew for certain was that Pete Richter had come after her. And he didn't seem like the kind of man who gave up easily.

Chapter Seventeen

A few hours later, Fiona lay on her bed—too tense to sleep or even to close her eyes. In those brief, terrifying seconds when she saw Richter running at her, he had a gun in his hand. If he'd wanted to kill her, he could have taken a shot. But he didn't fire his weapon. Instead, he charged from the shadows in a desperate attempt to do…what?

She knew well enough that bad things sometimes happen for no discernible reason, but that adage generally applied to natural disasters or car accidents or illnesses. People had motives. What did Richter want from her?

She rolled over to her side. For tonight, she felt safe. Jesse had deployed a team of bodyguards outside her house, and he was inside, wide awake. Through her partially opened bedroom door—a safety precaution in case Richter crashed through her window—she could hear him pacing in the front room.

Only a few hours ago, she'd been in his arms, kissing him and wanting him to make love to her. Her body still yearned for his touch.

She flipped onto her belly. Even if they didn't make love, she wanted to be with him. The way she felt about Jesse was more than hormones and passion. She trusted him. Within moments after they met, she'd told him her secrets. She truly believed that he'd keep her safe no matter what the threat. Damn it, what did Richter want from her?

The answer came to her in a flash. Simple.

Obvious. Why hadn't she thought of it before? She threw off the covers, grabbed her plaid flannel bathrobe, cinched the tie around the waist and went down the hall to tell Jesse.

He was waiting for her. He leaned against the sofa facing the hallway. His right hand rested on the butt of his sidearm, ready for action. His lean, muscular frame radiated strength. No bad guy in his right mind would mess with Jesse Longbridge.

He grinned at her. "What took you so long?"

"Do you think I can't stay away from you?"

"I think you want to talk. I could see it when you went off to bed. Actually, I was counting on it."

Because he wanted to make love to her? The hormonal urges that she'd put aside when alone in her bedroom rushed to the forefront of her mind. She totally forgot her brilliant yet obvious insight. "You were counting on me? To do what?"

"I need some practical help."

"P-p-practical?" If he was talking about love-making, that was a really odd description. "Isn't that kind of clinical?"

"It is." He unfastened the first button on his shirt. Then the second. His chest was smooth. His skin, vibrant. The color of a mocha latte. "I need some help changing the bandage on my shoulder."

He pivoted and strode into the kitchen, leaving her gaping. Mentally, she shook herself. He wanted her as his nurse not his lover. She trailed behind him, her wool socks shuffling on the hardwood floor.

On the kitchen counter, he'd laid out the necessary antiseptics, soap, bandages and towels. "I thought we should do it in here," he said. "The bathroom is right next to Abby's room, and I don't want to wake her."

"Are you planning on making a lot of noise?"

"That depends." He arched a suggestive eyebrow. "Will you be gentle?"

He was most definitely leading her on, and

she didn't mind being led. But she did have something important to say. "I figured out why Richter is after me."

"I thought you might come up with something." He unbuttoned the rest of his shirt. "You have the mind of an investigator. You're smart and creative. You can look at a problem and see all the possibilities."

He slipped off his shirt.

She struggled to maintain an air of detachment, to look at him as if he were one of the models she sculpted in art classes. His shoulders were wide, slightly out of proportion to his narrow hips. His torso wasn't overly muscled like a bodybuilder's, but his abs were nicely defined. There wasn't an ounce of flab on his torso. He was, in her opinion, a perfect male subject, worthy of Michelangelo.

She froze, unable to speak or think or do anything but stand and stare as he peeled off the adhesive and removed the gauze bandage.

Black sutures closed the jagged wound, leaving an angry red scar.

She stammered. "D-d-does it hurt?"

"Not the stitches. The wound is healing, but the muscles are still sore, especially when I lift my arm above my shoulder." He illustrated and winced. "Like that."

The muscles in his upper arm flexed as he raised his hand above his head and gave a new perspective to his body. She wished she had a camera to record his pose. Not that she'd ever forget this moment.

She thought of the various sculptures in her studio, each representing the way she'd been feeling at the time. The happy little houses. The angry trees. The empty vessels.

Jesse represented a new phase in her life. Sensual and strong.

"Fiona? Are you going to tell me what you figured out?"

She tore her gaze away from his torso and got

busy, grabbing a washcloth from the counter. "Let me get this cleaned up. Is this some kind of special soap?"

"I don't know. Wentworth said to use it."

She turned the water in the kitchen sink to hot, held the washcloth under it and worked the soap into a light lather. When she touched his chest, his flesh quivered. A corresponding shiver went through her. "When I came into the front room, you said you knew I wanted to talk. Why?"

"You had that look. When there's something going on inside your head, your eyebrows tilt up. And I was right, wasn't I?"

"How did you get to know me so well?" She carefully washed the area around his wound, holding her other hand at a clumsy angle to keep from touching his chest.

"The same way you know me. We have a connection."

"We do." And it was more than the link that

290 Bodyguard Under the Mistletoe

came when he saved her husband's life so many years ago. "It feels like we were meant to meet at this particular time and place."

"And walk the same path through life."

She wasn't so sure about that. "Your path is a lot more dangerous than mine."

"Not at the moment," he reminded her.

"Okay, here's what I figured out. You and Burke assumed that Richter was the one who rode into town and exchanged his horse for a car he bought from Silas O'Toole's grandson."

He nodded.

"What if it was Butch? Butch grabbed the ransom and stashed it someplace before he met up with his partner. That's why Richter killed him." She rinsed the washcloth in the sink and wiped away the soap on his shoulder. "Richter is coming after me because he thinks I know where Butch hid the money. Because of the secret room in my barn where Nicole was held, he thinks Butch and I were working together."

"Maybe he thought you and Butch were lovers."

"Eww."

"You saw those photos of Butch Thurgood. He was a rodeo star. A good-looking cowboy."

"Not my type." Her type was the man standing bare-chested in front of her. "Richter's suspicions are completely unfounded. They don't really have anything to do with me."

"It has everything to do with who you are," he said softly. "You're so pretty and sexy that even a snake like Richter assumes you have a lover."

"Oh, pul-eeze." With the towel, she patted his shoulder dry. "You make it sound like I'm some kind of sultry siren, luring cowboys to my ranch."

He stroked his fingers through her long hair and spread the tresses on either side of her face. "The new woman in town. The mysterious, desirable Widow Grant."

With a flip of his wrist, he unfastened the sash that held her robe together. His right hand slipped inside, circled her waist and yanked her toward him. The thin material of her jersey nightshirt pressed against his bare chest. Her body molded to his. She arched her neck, ready for his kiss.

Instead, he dipped his head and nuzzled her ear. His teeth caught her lobe and tugged, causing an electric spark.

Her hands glided across his bare back. Her fingertips savored the texture of his skin and the hard muscles beneath.

He held her firmly. One hand stroked her back. The other cupped her bottom and fitted her tightly against his hard erection. She ground her hips, pushing hard, pinning him against the kitchen counter.

His mouth was hot, demanding, passionate. As he kissed her, the spark ignited and fire surged through her veins. She clawed at his back, wanting him, needing him.

In a seemingly effortless move, he scooped her

off the floor and lifted her onto the countertop. Her thighs spread. Her bare legs wrapped around him as he peeled off her bathrobe.

She heard a sound outside the sphere of their passion.

Jesse reacted immediately. He separated from her, grabbed his gun and crept toward the back door.

She heard Wentworth's voice. "Open up. I'm freezing my tail off."

"Bad timing," Jesse muttered.

While he answered the door, she pulled herself together, fastening her robe and straightening her hair. There was nothing she could do about the heat pulsing through her. She knew her face was flushed and her eyes alit with passion.

Wentworth tromped into the kitchen, bringing the cold with him. His gaze focused on the floor, and he kept moving as he mumbled something about going to the bathroom.

She looked at Jesse—shirtless with a heavy

bulge in his crotch. It was ridiculously obvious what they'd been doing.

She grinned. "I think we embarrassed Wentworth."

"He'll get over it."

But their passion—no matter how urgent—would have to wait. Having guards on rotating shifts patrolling her house wasn't exactly conducive to intimacy.

"I'd like to finish what we started," she said. "And I'm not talking about your bandage."

He embraced her lightly and whispered, "I want to do this right, Fiona. To make love on satin sheets and spend the night holding you. I want your face to be my first sight in the morning."

She sighed and leaned her cheek against his bare chest. "Sounds perfect."

"I want to give you every luxury. All the special little things."

"Been there," she said.

"I know you have."

"Having a lot of things doesn't make you happy. I'm just as warm in faux fur as in a mink coat. And a whole lot more politically correct."

He stepped back and held her at arm's length. "Wyatt was a good man, a good provider, the father of your child."

She hadn't been thinking of Wyatt. His memory was just that: a precious memory. "I'll never forget him."

"He was the love of your life."

He turned away from her, went to the counter and started sorting through the surgical supplies. Though he had moved only a few paces away, it seemed that a gulf had opened between them. Did he resent her love for Wyatt? Was this going to be an issue?

Her feelings for Jesse were too new to understand or explain. She wouldn't call it love. Not yet, anyway. But when she was with him, she felt joy and hope and an indescribable glow.

"When Wyatt died," she said, "my life

didn't end. For a while, I wished that it had. It would have been easier for me to jump into the grave with him."

He turned toward her. "The grave that's right outside your front door."

She hadn't realized how omnipresent Wyatt was in her life, especially in this cabin. There was a photo of him on her bedside table. Abby's room was full of stuffed animals he'd bought for her. The radio was tuned to his favorite oldies station.

"My life is moving forward," she said.

Avoiding her gaze, he glanced down at the scar on his shoulder. "The stitches are almost healed. I don't think I need the big bandage."

He was changing the subject, avoiding an emotional land mine. Usually, Fiona insisted on expressing her feelings, but she was confused. It was better to get back to business. "Let me put on the antiseptic, and we'll finish with a couple of these extra-large patches."

As she tended to his shoulder, he looked away. She did the same.

They'd gone from blazing hot to icy. Back to business. Tersely, she asked, "What do you think of my theory about Richter?"

"Makes sense, but it doesn't explain the most important thing. What happened to Nicole?"

"According to Dylan, she's gone. She left him."

"Do you believe that?"

"Carolyn said they'd been arguing. Their marriage was already in trouble, but every couple has times like that." She and Wyatt had their share of spats. Good grief, was she thinking about him again? She placed the bandage on Jesse's shoulder and stepped back. "Whatever Nicole said to him was enough to convince Dylan. He believes that she wants a divorce."

He slipped back into his shirt. "When I hear those words from her lips, I'll believe it, too. For now, she's still my client. I need to know that she's safe."

"Do you think Richter is still holding her?"

"Don't know." He took the bottled water and sat at the kitchen table. His long legs stretched out in front of him.

He looked tired, as if the exertions of the day had finally caught up with him. And she wanted to help, to make him feel better. "Are there other leads to follow?"

"Tomorrow morning, I'll start tracking again. This time, I'll start at the place where Nicole and Dylan met."

"At the same time as the ransom was being delivered," she said. "Can I come with you?"

"No." The merest hint of a smile flickered at the corner of his lips. "You're my client, too. I intend to keep you and Abby under guard."

"Richter wouldn't dare come after me if I was with you."

"No? The last time I tangled with Pete Richter, he nearly killed me. He shot first. And I failed at my job."

"You didn't fail." A frustrated sigh pushed through her lips. "This is the last time I'm going to say this—the kidnapping wasn't your fault."

"Tell that to Nicole."

She thought of the tiny secret room where Nicole had been held prisoner, tethered to the bed with a chain, unable to see the daylight. In the proof-of-life videos, she looked strong and upbeat. But she must have been scared.

The natural empathy she felt for Nicole extended to Jesse. He, too, was suffering. He'd taken on the entire responsibility for what had happened, called himself a failure.

She knew that he had ghosts of his own. She asked, "What happened in Telluride?"

His jaw tensed. She knew it was difficult for him to speak of the incident he'd referred to as a mistake. "I never should have brought that up."

"But you did." She sat at the table. "You told me because you feel like you can trust me. I want that, Jesse. I want to understand you."

"I'm not complicated."

"The hell you aren't." She took his hand. "Tell me."

He exhaled in a whoosh. "Private lodge in Telluride. A CEO, his two teenaged daughters and his wife."

"Were they all skiing?"

"Not the wife. She preferred staying home, reading a book or knitting. A nice woman. I'll never forget the look in her eyes when I told her that her husband had been shot."

Fiona suppressed a gasp. "What happened?"

"The daughters weren't hurt. And their father survived. Barely." He squeezed her hand. "I didn't see the sniper in the trees. Not until it was too late."

She wanted to reassure him, to tell him that he must have done the best he could. But she knew the stark, haunted expression in his dark eyes would not be easily assuaged. His pain was too deep. "You're in a rough business."

"And failure has deadly results. I won't rest until I find Nicole."

Chapter Eighteen

The next morning, Jesse planned to leave Fiona's house early and drive to the Carlisle Ranch, where he'd meet up with Burke and follow the second kidnapper's tracks, much as they'd done yesterday.

He finished brushing his teeth and left the bathroom. In the back of his mind, he was kind of hoping to skate out the door without saying too much to Fiona. He wouldn't purposely avoid her; that would be cowardly. But their talk last night raked up bad memories of a time when he'd almost lost a client. Painful, but he could cope. He'd had years to deal with that failure.

What he couldn't handle was their intimacy—the taste of her kiss, the pressure of her slender body against his, the silky texture of her long hair, her scent and her sighs. His desire for her opened a whole new arena of regret. He connected with her. From the moment they met, he had a sense that she was the woman he wanted at his side as he walked through life. But she'd already found her one true love in Wyatt Grant, and Jesse could never replace him. Falling in love with Fiona would only break his heart.

Steeling himself to face her, he strode into the kitchen. Abby was at the kitchen table, chatting happily with one of the ranch hands who had spent the night on patrol. Jesse gave the young man a nod. "MacKenzie."

He nodded back. "Morning, Jesse."

Abby bounced down from her chair, took his

hand and led him toward the counter. "Come here. Right now. You need coffee."

He followed the bossy, little blonde pixie. "And why are you so sure of that?"

She rolled her baby-blue eyes. "Everybody is sooo tired today."

"I suppose you're right." After a night of rotating shifts with the other men guarding her house, he'd gotten barely enough sleep. And his dreams had been troubled.

"You have to pour it yourself," Abby said as she went to the refrigerator. "I'm not allowed to touch hot stuff, but I can get the milk."

She held the nearly empty container up to him. Though he usually took his coffee black, he added a dollop of milk. "Thank you, Abby."

"I'm a very good hostess."

"You took good care of me."

"I know," she said. "And I would take very good care of a pony."

"Would you give him coffee?"

"Silly." She laughed. "Ponies eat oatmeal."

As she flounced back to the table, he helped himself to a blueberry muffin. No fruit this morning. Food supplies were running low. Later today, somebody would need to make a run to the market.

He gulped down the coffee and ate the muffin over the sink. If he moved fast, he could make his escape without running into Fiona. To Mac-Kenzie, he said, "I'm heading out. Tell Wentworth that I'll be back by noon."

He was unlocking the back door when he heard Fiona's voice behind his shoulder. "Were you going to leave without saying goodbye?"

He turned. Caught. "Goodbye."

She looked rested and alert with a touch of makeup on her wide gray eyes and a glossy pink lipstick. Her shiny brown hair hung in a neat braid down her back.

"Not so fast," she said. "I'd like your opinion on one of the pieces I fired in the kiln last night."

"Can't help you." He gazed longingly at the door. "I don't know much about art."

Much like Abby, she took his hand and pulled him down the hallway to her studio. The females in this family had a definite bossy streak. "My inspiration for this piece was the Navajo wedding vase."

The interior of her studio was transformed. The last time he was in here, sketch pads and tools were piled on the worktable. Now that space held a neat display of finished artworks—small sculptures of bright-colored houses, exotic plants, strange-looking creatures and a variety of pots and vases.

"I liked the idea of the wedding vase," she said. "With two spouts rising from the same vessel. Separate but joined together."

A pearly glaze shimmered on a pot that seemed to be made of leaves. Wintery but not cold. Her talent impressed him, but her words sank deep. *Separate but joined together.* A marriage didn't have to be all-consuming. He touched the pearly ceramic. "It's like living ice."

She beamed. "You like it."

"I like all of it." Some of the odd little animals made him smile. The shapes on the pots were fascinating. "You're good."

"Andrea—Carolyn and Dylan's mother—is coming over this morning. She owns a gallery in Manhattan. If I can convince her to show my work, I gain instant credibility."

With the way she wore her heart on her sleeve, he should have expected this creative side to her personality. She was one of the most expressive people he'd ever known. Every minute he spent in her company fascinated him and drew him closer. "Andrea would be a fool not to show your work."

She went up on tiptoe and gave him a quick peck on the cheek. "That's what I needed to hear. Now you can go."

Now he wanted to stay. He picked up one of

the pots—a simple, functional shape with a geometric design of orange and deep blue. "This reminds me of some of the Navajo artists. My grandfather would have liked it."

"That's a terrific compliment. I know how important he was to you."

Jesse remembered. "I dreamed about him last night. I saw him walking across a high mesa. There was a woman with him. A blonde woman."

"Nicole," she said.

"I called her name, and I raced toward them, leaping from one rock to another. But I didn't get any closer. You know how that is? Running in a dream?"

"I know."

"My grandfather came to the edge of the cliff and raised both arms to a glaring sun. The light flared. Nicole was gone."

He feared for her, feared that Richter had killed her and left her body in a shallow grave.

Searching these mountains would take months, even years. They might never find her body.

"What does it mean?" she asked.

He wouldn't voice that fear, wouldn't give it substance by saying it aloud. "When my grandfather turned around, I was next to him. Close enough to touch the leather medicine pouch that hung from his neck, but I didn't reach toward him."

Though he didn't believe the lore about ghost-walkers and shape-shifters, he respected the dead. "He spoke to me in Navajo. I don't understand the language very well, but I knew what he was saying. 'Follow your path.'"

"Like the trail you followed into town," she said. "Maybe he was telling you that you're on the right track."

Jesse frowned. He didn't know what the hell his dream meant. He was tired of riddles and pieces of clues. He wanted to know exactly what to do next. "I should go."

"I'll be here waiting."

Whether he liked it or not, he knew that his path would always lead back to Fiona.

AT THE CARLISLE RANCH, Jesse didn't bother going inside. He went directly to the stables. The bay horse he'd been riding yesterday nickered when he came close to his stall. He was a good mount, even-tempered and sensitive to direction. Within a few minutes, Jesse was saddled up and ready to go.

Outside the stable, another rider was waiting. "Need some help?"

It was Dylan. A mantle of anger and grief still draped around him, but there was a different energy as well—a sense of determination.

"How are you at tracking?" Jesse asked.

"Pretty good. I'm a hunter." He nodded back toward the house. "Burke won't be joining us. He got a lead on the whereabouts of Zeke O'Toole."

Jesse flicked his reins. "Let's see what we can find."

Together, they set out across the south pasture. Jesse didn't need directions to the creek where Nicole had met with her husband. It was near the same place Jesse had witnessed the actual kidnapping—the place where he'd been shot.

To their east, a panorama of ranch land, valley and rolling hills stretched toward distant snow-capped peaks. Wispy clouds streaked the blue skies, and sunlight brightened the khaki winter fields. Though he couldn't help but marvel at the vast beauty of this land bordering the edge of the forest, Jesse had a sense of foreboding. Dylan must have been feeling much the same way. At this quiet glen in the forest, his wife had told him their marriage was over.

He glanced toward the man riding beside him. In his shearling jacket and fawn-colored Stetson, Dylan Carlisle was one-hundred-percent cowboy. He'd lived on this land all his life; the acreage and cattle belonged to his family. A heavy responsibility.

When Dylan first hired Longbridge Security—only hours before the kidnapping— he'd been tense. His ranch was under assault from vandals who had burned down an old stable. Though he didn't like the idea that he needed bodyguards for protection, he wasn't rude or arrogant.

The last time they met, Dylan had lashed out at him. *Justifiably,* Jesse thought. Still, it hadn't been Dylan's finest hour.

They slowed as they reached the winding path that led to a stream. In springtime, this trail would have been green and beautiful. Now the white branches of aspens were skeletal and bare. The shrubs were brown, spiky clumps.

Jesse ignored his memory of being shot. They were here to find out what had happened after Dylan met Nicole. Earlier, the cowboy accepted her at her word; he had refused to search for his wife.

"What changed your mind?" Jesse asked.

"Burke told me about what you'd found yesterday. The trail that went into Riverton. Buying a car from Zeke." He shook his head. "This kidnapping plot is more complicated than I thought. Butch is dead. And why is Richter still hanging around?"

"Got to be the money," Jesse said. "Are you thinking we might be able to get the ransom back?"

"I don't give a damn about the ransom." He reined his horse beside the trickling stream. "Here's where she met me."

He stared hard at an empty space in front of a tall spruce. His jaw tightened. Though Jesse could tell that Dylan wasn't a man given to emotional display, he saw a tear spill down his cheek.

He continued. "It wasn't the first time Nicole told me off. We're going through a rough patch in our marriage. Trying to get pregnant. When she said she wanted a divorce, I believed her. And now…" He cleared his throat. "Now I'm thinking I might have been wrong. That she's still out there being held prisoner."

Or worse. Not a thought Jesse wanted to dwell on. "Let's see what we can find."

"A couple of my men were already out here," Dylan said. "They picked up a trail that led toward Fiona's house."

"One rider?"

Dylan nodded.

Jesse was pretty sure that wasn't right. There should have been two sets of tracks. His assumption was that Nicole had been accompanied by one of the kidnappers. Why else would they split up?

One of them grabbed the ransom and rode into town. The other stayed with Nicole. He sat up in his saddle and scanned the surrounding forest. "I'm guessing that she didn't come to this meeting alone. One of the kidnappers was with her, maybe holding a gun on her."

"You think she was coerced? That they threatened to shoot her if she didn't say what they wanted?"

Dylan drew that conclusion quickly. He must have already been considering the possibility that Nicole was acting under duress.

"You're a hunter," Jesse said. "If you wanted a clear shot at this spot, where would you hide?"

"Uphill. It was just after dark when I met her. There are plenty of places he could have been hiding in the trees."

"Leave the horses here." Jesse dismounted. "I'll go left. You go right."

He climbed slowly, taking note of every broken twig, every mark on the ground. The stream attracted more than kidnappers and victims. There were hoofprints from elk. At the base of a pine tree, he found a squirrel's cache stuffed with pinecones.

"Found a boot print," Dylan called out.

The vantage point where Dylan stood was uphill. A sniper in that position would have had a clear shot at Nicole, unless she made a sudden break and raced toward the ranch. She was a good rider, experienced enough to know that she could have escaped, especially since the kidnapper wasn't on horseback.

The beginning of an idea began to take shape in his mind. "Be there in a minute."

He found what he was looking for. A neat set of boot prints behind a tree. His horse had been only a couple of yards away, hidden behind a boulder.

There were two kidnappers watching Nicole, holding a gun on her. Two at this spot. Another at La Rana to pick up the ransom.

Butch and Richter had help.

Chapter Nineteen

When Fiona welcomed Andrea into her house, she was fully aware that this meeting could change her career.

The sophisticated Manhattanite greeted her and Abby with warm hugs. Gazing around the front room, Andrea said, "I haven't been in this house for years. Over twenty years, in fact. Sterling and I used to play cards with the Grants."

"Wyatt's parents," Fiona said. She found it hard to believe that Andrea was part of a prior generation. She didn't look older than forty. And a fabulous forty, at that.

"We used to laugh all night. Drink gallons of wine and ride home singing at the top of our lungs." Her voice was tinged with nostalgia. "Not many people knew that side of Sterling Carlisle. Everyone saw him as the patriarch, the founder of Carlisle Certified Organic Beef."

"And now your children are carrying on his legacy. You must be proud of them."

"Proud? Yes. Also worried."

How could she not be worried? She'd returned to a ranch in the midst of trauma. Fiona placed a sympathetic hand on her shoulder. "Would you like a cup of tea?"

The only coffee Fiona had left was instant. Her food supplies were running low after feeding all the bodyguards and search teams that had descended upon her house.

"Nothing for me," Andrea said. "With the

way Polly has been feeding me, I'll never fit into my clothes when I get back to New York."

"She's an amazing cook," Fiona agreed.

Abby piped up, "Polly gives me cookies."

There had been a time when Fiona would have been gushing with apologies and embarrassed about the lack of fresh ground coffee and the less than pristine condition of her home. During her marriage, she'd taken her duties as a hostess seriously, knowing that Wyatt would be judged on her performance. If Fiona's hemline had been too short or if she'd served the wrong wine with dinner or if she laughed too loudly, people would talk.

Now she was free to be herself, and she liked the feeling. *A fresh start.* Jesse had mentioned walking together on a new path, discovering new adventures. That was the route she wanted to take.

Abby rushed to the dining room and climbed onto a chair. She pointed to the colorfully painted Santa Claus ceramic centerpiece. "I made this."

"It's lovely," Andrea said.

"Mommy says we're going to get a Christmas tree pretty soon and decorate."

"And what do you want from Santa?"

"A pony," Abby said quickly.

Fiona lifted her daughter off her perch and settled the child onto her hip. Though Abby was almost too heavy to carried, she couldn't be allowed to run free in the studio—not while there were so many pieces on display, tempting Abby to touch.

Fiona unlocked the studio door, ushered Andrea inside and got out of the way. Her artwork needed to speak for itself. There was nothing Fiona could say to convince an experienced dealer like Andrea to give her a chance.

Abby, on the other hand, was bursting with comments about the fairy houses and animals and big pots.

While Andrea viewed the many objects on display, her eyes were hard and analytical. "You have talent, Fiona. And imagination. I've seldom seen such a wide range of pottery and sculpture."

Fiona listened for the "but." *Talented, but... Skillful, but...*

Andrea continued. "You're an emotional artist. I can see your happiness. Your anger. And your fear."

But...

"I'd like to show your work. In late spring, I've arranged for a couple of other sculptors." She mentioned an impressive list of artists. "Your pottery would fit in quite well."

She gave Abby a squeeze. Their financial situation was about to take a turn for the better. She couldn't wait to tell Jesse. "Thanks so much."

"We'll work out the details," Andrea said. "Why don't you and Abby come home with me? I'm sure it'll be easier for all of us to be guarded at the same time. We have plenty of food. And coffee."

"And horses," Abby said.

Fiona whipped out her cell phone. "I need to check with Jesse first, but I'm sure it'll be okay."

She wanted to believe that everything would turn out well. It felt as though the tide had turned, and luck was on her side.

AT THE CARLISLE RANCH house, Fiona and Abby were well protected. All the ranch hands who weren't actually working the cattle were armed and assigned to guard duty.

After lunch, she and Abby took a walk toward the stable with Carolyn. Fiona said, "It looks like the Old West around here. All these cowboys with rifles."

"The amazing thing," Carolyn said, "is that most of these guys are even less enlightened than their 1800s counterparts."

"Yeah, yeah, yeah. I know you love this ranch."

"But my home is in Denver." She tipped her cowboy hat back on her forehead. "I can't wait to get back to my high-rise condo with the Jacuzzi bathtub and the walk-in closet. I have a pair of designer stilettos in acrylic and silver that I've never worn."

"Not to mention the extra benefit," Fiona said. "Burke lives in the city. Is he more enlightened than a cowboy?"

"I have tickets for *The Nutcracker* next week, and he agreed to go with me."

"To the ballet?" Fiona had a hard time imagining the big, rugged FBI agent sitting still for an evening of Tchaikovsky and tutus.

"He promised. And the ballet is where I'm going to wear those stilettos for the first time."

Fiona appreciated the irony of discussing ballet and designer shoes on her way to the stable with a woman who was dressed like the archetypal cowgirl in jeans and dusty boots.

They reached the corral where Carolyn's

horse, Elvis, greeted them with a toss of his head. She lifted Abby onto the second from the top rail on the fence so she could reach across and pet the horse.

"I love Elvis," Abby said. "What are stilettos?"

"Shoes with pointy heels. You've seen the ones I have."

"You don't wear them anymore."

And she didn't miss them. The realization hit her that she was happy living here, running around in sneakers, climbing the hills and breathing the mountain air. Even if she became a successful potter with a display in Manhattan, she'd choose to live here.

Looking out across the south pasture, she saw two men riding toward them. Jesse was in front, leaning forward in a gallop. The unexpected sight of him took her breath away. On horseback, he looked powerful and incredibly masculine. No matter what Carolyn said, cowboys were sexy.

Carolyn nudged her shoulder. "Is there something going on with you and Jesse?"

"I hope so."

She should probably be guarded about what
she said around Abby, but Fiona had never been
able to hide her feelings. She was drawn to
Jesse as a friend, a protector and—please,
God!—a lover.

Abby waved with both hands. "Jesse! I'm
over here."

He rode up beside the corral fence. "I see
you, Abby."

"Did you catch the bad guys?"

"Not yet." He leaned down and lifted the little
girl off the fence onto the saddle in front of him.
"But I caught you."

Fiona liked the way he swooped in and took
charge, walking his horse in a wide arc while
Abby held the reins and chatted at a million
miles an hour.

Dylan, who had been riding with Jesse, dismounted beside them. He turned toward his sister. "I might have been mistaken about Nicole."

"You? Wrong?" Carolyn looked up toward the sky and squinted. "What's that I see? A pig flying?"

"We don't have time for jokes," he said. "Where's Burke?"

"In the house."

"Take care of my horse." He tossed the reins toward her and stalked toward the ranch house.

As Carolyn watched him, the grin faded from her face. "He's so much like our father. Stubborn. It'd serve him right if Nicole never came back to him."

"You don't mean that," Fiona said.

"Of course I don't."

But the ongoing stress showed in her eyes. Everyone at the ranch was trying to maintain calm, but an undercurrent of dread tinted every conversation. They couldn't help worrying about Nicole, couldn't help fearing the worst.

Fiona's cell phone rang, and she answered. It was Belinda with a request. She had the chance to take another shift at the café and hoped Fiona could take of Mickey for a few hours. "I wouldn't ask, but I really need the money."

Fiona checked with Carolyn, who nodded and said, "I think we can make room for one little boy."

"Here's the deal," Fiona said into the phone. "Abby and I are staying at the Carlisle Ranch, and Carolyn says it's okay for Mickey to come here."

"The Carlisle Ranch? Wow." Belinda paused. "If Nate ever found out that his son visited the Carlisles, he'd explode."

"Is that a problem?" Fiona asked.

"Not for me."

She could hear the smile in Belinda's voice. "See you at four."

Jesse dismounted with Abby tucked under his arm and placed her on the ground. When he stood, his gaze linked with Fiona's. A burst of excitement surged inside her. She hadn't told him about Andrea yet, about new possibilities.

"You two can talk," Carolyn said as she took Abby's hand. "We cowgirls need to go into the stable and tend to the horses."

"Really?" Abby skipped beside her. "Can I help?"

"Only if you do exactly as I say. Got it?"

Jesse leaned against the corral fence. His boot heel hooked on the lowest rung. He took off his hat, smoothed his black hair and put it back on. "We found evidence that there was a third person involved in the kidnapping."

Her news about Andrea would have to wait. This was big. "Tell me."

"At the place by the stream where Dylan met Nicole, we found two sets of prints. Two men. They were positioned in such a way that they had a clear shot at both Nicole and Dylan."

Fiona understood immediately. "They threatened her. If she hadn't told Dylan those things, they would have killed both her and Dylan."

The kidnappers' threat had produced the effect they wanted. Dylan had been convinced by Nicole's performance, and he called off the search for her.

"After she talked to Dylan, Nicole rode south. Near your house, she was joined by both men. They rode to a graded dirt road. We couldn't find tire marks, but a car must have been parked there."

"Zeke O'Toole's car," she said.

He nodded. "I'm assuming that one of them drove into town to hook up with the third man. He's the one who was holding the ransom."

"And where was Nicole?"

"She had to be in the car. Tracks showed that the kidnapper who had been left behind rode to the Circle M to return the three horses. Two horses were riderless."

She hung on every word of his explanation.

It amazed her that he'd discovered so much from tracking. "Then what happened?"

"The trail stops there. We don't know what happened next, but I'm assuming two of the men—probable Butch and Richter—came back here, and you heard them arguing."

Once again, the clues had led to her house. "Why here? What were they looking for?"

He shrugged. "I've been asking myself the same question. And I don't have an answer."

"If the sheriff was here, he'd probably tell you that they rode back toward my house because I'm the mastermind of the whole kidnapping scheme."

"Sheriff Trainer has some explaining to do," he said. "Dylan and I found these tracks. Why didn't he?"

"Maybe he didn't know where to look."

"That's what Dylan said. None of the other trackers thought to look up higher on the hillside, to check possible sniper positions."

"You're a better tracker than they are."

"I'm not a genius," he protested.

She reached toward him, and pointed her forefinger, counting each of the buttons on his shirt. "But you're good. Very good. Better than average."

"And how do you know that?"

"Intuition."

A slow grin spread across his face. God, he was handsome. His voice was low and sexy as he asked, "What else does your intuition tell you?"

That we're meant to be together. That you're the man I'm meant to spend the rest of my life with. It'd be crazy to blurt out that kind of declaration. They'd only known each other for a matter of days—not long enough make a life-changing decision. She'd only just decided that she might be interested in sex. Making plans for the future? She wasn't ready to take that giant step.

"My intuition says…" she dropped her

voice "…that we should make love as soon as possible."

"I'll put it on my schedule," he said. "Right after I protect you from a deranged killer, rescue Nicole, and find the ransom."

"If we wait too long, you'll be gone."

"Maybe not."

She couldn't guess what that meant. That he intended to spend a little more time here? How long? Where would he stay?

It was all too complicated.

She changed the subject. "Andrea liked my sculptures and pots. I'm going to display in her gallery."

"Good news." He gave her a huge hug, lifting her off her feet and spinning her around. "You're the genius."

She laughed. "I'll settle for good enough to start selling."

"Does that mean you're packing up your kiln and moving to New York?"

"No way." The sky behind him was a pure, deep blue. The winter air felt crisp. "This is home."

When he kissed her, it felt good and right.

How long would she have to wait before they finally made love?

How many days should it take for her to tell him that she'd fallen in love with him at first sight?

Chapter Twenty

After a couple of hours in the dining room with the high-powered threesome of Burke, Dylan and Carolyn, Jesse needed a break. He went outside and stood on the veranda. Afternoon shadows spread across the landscape. Sunset was only a couple of hours away. It would be another night with Nicole missing.

The discovery of a third person working with Butch and Richter put a different spin on their investigation. He'd listened to the different strategies, theories and plans from Burke and the two Carlisles. He'd looked at the maps they laid out, reviewed the prior case notes. Nothing in particular resonated.

Thus far, he'd had success as a tracker. Now his instincts told him that it was time to hunt, time for battle. His wounds had healed enough to take on a fight. Damn it, he was ready to kick ass. But whose ass needed kicking? Who was the third man working with Richter and Butch?

Fiona came out of the house and joined him. She rested her forearms on the railing, arched her back like a cat and stretched. Her round bottom presented an enticing target.

She said, "Abby's busy in the kitchen, making cookies with Polly. I thought I'd catch up on the investigation."

"You're asking the wrong guy," he said, still studying her rear end. "I tuned out."

"Come on, Jesse. I want to know."

"And I want to…"

When he playfully squeezed her bottom, she

stood up straight and flashed him a grin. "I can't believe you did that."

"No apology. You were asking for it, waving a red flag in front of a bull."

"Okay, Mr. Bull." She twitched her hips. "You've been in the dining room for hours. You must have come up with something."

"Burke's working his cell phone. Carolyn and Dylan are mostly growling at each other."

"They argue a lot," she said. "Strong opinions on both sides."

And not many answers. With a dearth of tangible leads and Richter disappearing into the forest like a jackrabbit, they had to go back to the beginning, starting with the question: who would want to kidnap Nicole? The wealthy, powerful Carlisle family had offended a lot of people over the years. There was a long list of enemies to consider.

"Dylan wants Burke to call in the FBI again." Which Jesse considered a desperate move. "He's not thinking straight. Going door to door and asking questions isn't going to find his wife."

She cocked her head and looked up at him. "Do you have a better idea?"

"Patience."

As he watched, a cowboy on horseback came from the stables at the rear of the house and rode to the front gate. He wore a gun at his hip and carried a rifle. At the main road, he relieved the guard on duty. Neat. Efficient.

Under Wentworth's supervision, the security at the Carlisle Ranch—using a combination of ranch hands and Longbridge Security employees—was excellent. Not quite military precision but close enough. Jesse owed his old friend a raise in pay. Or maybe a few weeks' paid vacation. *As if that pays him back for saving my life?*

Beside him, she fidgeted. "I have to ask. Patience? What does that mean?"

"The hardest part of hunting is waiting.

We've gathered information. Now we wait for the pieces to fall into place. We need one last clue that will make sense of everything."

"Everything?" Her voice was skeptical.

"It's not that complicated."

"Then how do you explain the secret room in my barn?" She held up her index finger. "That's my first question. Number two, who killed Butch Thurgood? Three, who bought Zeke O'Toole's car and why? Four, who's the third man?"

She waved her four fingers in front of his eyes, and he caught hold of her hand. "The only important questions are, Where's Nicole? Where's the ransom?"

Her fingers laced with his and she leaned closer. "How long? How long before all these questions are answered?"

"One explanation will lead to another. Our best lead is Zeke O'Toole. Burke put out a BOLO with the state police."

"BOLO?"

"Be On the Look-Out," he explained. "When we find Zeke and find out who he sold his car to, we'll have answers."

She glanced down. When she looked up again, her eyes gleamed like silver. "I've never been good at waiting."

"It's all part of the hunt." He raised her hand and brushed his lips across her knuckles. It was becoming increasingly difficult to keep his hands off her. "You have to know when to take action. And when to hold back."

Her voice lowered to a sultry whisper. "We're not talking about the investigation anymore, are we?"

"You know what I'm talking about."

"I want you, too."

Everything about her excited him. The curve of her full lips. The way her chin lifted when she smiled. He wanted to make love to her right now. She was sexy and sassy and had made it damn clear that she was ready.

But he wanted more from Fiona than a one-night stand. He wanted a commitment. They were meant to be together; he'd sensed their connection the first time he saw her.

Thinking back to that time, he smiled. Was it only three days ago? Her appearance was so different from when they met. Before, she was waiflike and fragile. "You've changed in the past few days."

"How so?"

He stepped back and framed her with his hands, as if taking her picture. "You've always shown your emotions. Now you own them. You're confident."

Her eyes widened in surprise. "How did you get to be so perceptive?"

"I think I've told you—about a hundred times—that I need to be able to read people in my line of work."

She moved closer again. Her hand rested against his chest. "What am I thinking right now?"

Her body language was clear. This was a woman who wanted kissing. She was filled with sensual longing. Ripe.

"If we were alone," he murmured, "I could tell you what I see. And what I want. But those words are going to have to wait."

"Why?"

He pointed toward the front gate. Belinda's aged station wagon turned toward the house. She waved to the guard and drove forward.

Fiona straightened her jacket. "I'm glad Mickey's here. Abby has been driving Polly crazy in the kitchen."

Belinda pulled into the parking area and got out of the car. Mickey dashed ahead of her and jumped up the steps to the veranda. "My daddy has a ranch."

"Yes, he does," Fiona said.

"And horses." Mickey puffed out his chest.

Belinda came up behind him. "I really appreciate this, Fiona. Do you think I could run inside and thank Carolyn?"

"Sure."

Jesse held the door and followed them inside. Mickey disappeared into the kitchen, where he and Abby greeted each other loudly. Belinda and Fiona went to the dining room.

Carolyn sat at the head of the dining-room table while her brother paced behind her. Dylan paused when they entered the room and looked toward them. Both Carlisles were striking— tall with black hair and pale green eyes.

As the shapely Belinda, wearing her fringed jacket, black slacks and waitress shoes, approached them, Jesse was reminded of a maidservant approaching royalty. In a way, that's what Carolyn and Dylan were—the inheritors of an empire, a multimillion-dollar, international business.

Intimidated, Belinda almost bowed as she came closer.

Fiona pulled her friend forward. "Carolyn and Dylan, I'd like to introduce Belinda Miller."

"Nate's wife?" Dylan barked.

"Not anymore," Fiona said smoothly.

"Divorced," he said. "I remember something about a restraining order."

"That's enough," Carolyn snapped at him as she rose from the chair and shook Belinda's hand. "Please excuse my brother. He's has the social graces of a jackass."

"Thanks so much for letting my son come over." Belinda's voice was hesitant. "Like I said to Fiona, I need all the work I can get with Christmas right around the corner."

"Belinda works at the café in Riverton," Fiona said. "And that gives me an idea. Everybody in town comes through the café. Belinda could keep an eye out for us. You know, a BOLO."

"I'd like to help out," Belinda said. "I feel terrible about Nicole. She helped me and Mickey rescue a stray dog that got hit by a car. Nicole's got a big heart."

When she mentioned Nicole, Dylan scowled

344 *Bodyguard Under the Mistletoe*

and folded his arms across his chest. He looked angry and imperious, but Jesse saw deeper. Dylan was coming to realize how little he knew about his wife. Nicole had taken the time to be friends with this woman, and Dylan didn't even know her name.

"First thing," Fiona said. "Do you know Zeke O'Toole?"

"Silas O'Toole's grandson? Sure, I know him. A cheapskate, just like his grandpa. Why on earth do you care about him?"

"He might have sold his car to the kidnappers," Fiona said.

Jesse liked the idea of using Belinda's natural contacts. He asked the next question. "How about Pete Richter? Have you ever met him?"

Belinda's chewed her lower lip. "I'm not sure. The Sons of Freedom guys didn't come to the café often. More likely, they were at the tavern."

"There's a photo of Richter on the computer," Fiona said.

Carolyn flipped the laptop with the case file around so Belinda could see. She tapped a few keys. "The mug shots should be in one of the photo files."

But the image that appeared on the screen was Nicole in a proof-of-life photo. In the background was a pale yellow sheet they now knew had been hung on the wall in the secret room under Fiona's barn. Nicole held the newspaper for the day following her kidnapping. The collar of her flowered cotton shirt seemed to emphasize the paleness of her skin. But her jaw was set, and her eyes showed fierce determination.

Belinda gasped. Her hand flew to cover her mouth. "That's after she was kidnapped."

"Sorry," Carolyn said. "Wrong file."

She flipped to the mug shots, zeroed in on the photo of Richter and made it full screen. "This is Richter."

Nervously, Belinda shook her head. "I don't recognize him. But I'll watch for him."

Burke charged into the room, holding his cell phone aloft like the Olympic torch. "They found the car. Sheriff Trainer found it abandoned outside town."

Inside, there would be a wealthy of forensic evidence. Fingerprints. Hairs. Traces.

This investigation was drawing to a close.

AFTER A SHOWER in Silas O'Toole's bathroom, Pete Richter got dressed fast. The clothes he found in Zeke's room fit him just fine. Zeke had a fine collection of Western-style shirts with pearl snaps. Richter chose one with a black yoke. He was glad to get rid of the clothes he'd been wearing for days. Even the squirrels could smell him coming.

After he fastened his holster on his hip and his hand ax on the other side, he put on fresh socks and his boots. Soon, he'd be able to afford everything new. Soon, the ransom would be his. After all he'd gone through, he damn well deserved that money.

He sauntered out of the bedroom and walked through Silas O'Toole's filthy house. The old man had money; he should have hired a woman to clean up this dump and cook some decent food. The only thing in the fridge was baloney and white bread.

He stood in the kitchen doorway and stared hard at his captive. Richter had grabbed Zeke as soon as the punk walked through the front door a half hour ago. His plan had been to make the kid talk right away and get the hell out of there. But he'd been a little too aggressive with his questions, and Zeke passed out. He'd been sitting here, tied to the kitchen chair with duct tape over his mouth, while Richter changed his clothes and got ready to start his new life.

"You're awake," Richter growled.

Zeke's eyes were scared. Blood matted the dirty blond hair on the side of his head.

"If you tell me what I want to know,"

Richter said, "I won't have to kill you. Understand?"

Zeke nodded.

This was going to be easy. Richter had wasted days trying to nab Fiona Grant. When he overheard one of those bodyguards talking about the getaway car, he almost kicked himself. He hadn't known the car was newly purchased from Zeke O'Toole when he stuffed Nicole into the trunk and drove to the meeting place. All Richter had been thinking about was following the plan he and Butch had been told over the phone.

He'd been stupid to trust the guy who gave them those orders. At first, he'd thought it was one of the guys from the SOF, maybe even Logan himself. He was wrong. All those boys had been rounded up by the FBI.

Then he figured it might be one of the ranch hands at the Carlisle place. One of them had been working with Logan.

Or it could have been somebody from town.

Or one of the sheriff's men, even Sheriff Trainer himself.

When he couldn't figure it out, he settled on Fiona as his best source of information.

Zeke was better. He knew something for sure.

Richter ripped the duct tape off his mouth. The kid took a giant gulp of air.

"About a week ago," Richter said, "you sold one of your piece-of-crap cars for cash. Who bought it?"

"If I tell you, he'll kill me."

Richter took the hand ax from his belt. "I'll do worse than kill you, Zeke."

The kid was almost crying. "I didn't do nothing."

Richter held the sharp edge of his ax under his nose and pushed his head back. "Maybe I'll break all your teeth. You won't look good to the ladies without a smile."

Richter took a step back and buried the ax

blade in the kitchen table. "And you are going to tell me."

"I'll talk. Don't hurt me."

And when he did, Richter wasn't too surprised.

Chapter Twenty-One

While Burke and Dylan headed off to meet with Sheriff Trainer at the site where they'd found the car, Fiona and Carolyn roamed around the dining-room table, picking through bits of shifting evidence.

Fiona scanned a map where the routes of the three kidnappers were drawn with dotted lines. *Patience.* Jesse had counseled patience. How long before these lines converged into a pattern? How much time did Nicole have left?

From the kitchen, she heard Jesse talking to the

kids, who were both trying to convince him and Polly that one cookie wouldn't spoil their dinner.

Andrea slipped into the dining room and greeted them both. Her manicured hand trembled as she touched her daughter's shoulder. "Do you have any news about Nicole?"

"The sheriff found the car that belonged to Zeke O'Toole," Carolyn said. "There were a couple of blond hairs in the trunk."

"The trunk? Dear Lord." Andrea sank into a chair at the table. "Anything else?"

"Dylan and Burke went to check out the car while they look for fingerprints and trace evidence."

The argument in the kitchen reached a crescendo with both children shouting "please" at the top of their lungs. Andrea glanced toward the racket, then smiled at Fiona. "I'm assuming one of those voices is Abby. Is there another child with her?"

"Mickey Miller," Fiona said.

"Miller? As in Nate Miller's son?"

"That's right," Carolyn said. "And you don't need to remind me of the feud between the Carlisles and the Millers that's been going on forever. Mickey's mother has nothing to do with Nate. She seems like a nice woman."

"You'll get no argument from me. I never understood why your father and Nate's father hated each other so much—other than the obvious fact that Miller was a truly unpleasant individual."

"Nate's the same way," Carolyn said. "Cranky and foul-tempered. He's on our list of suspects. In fact, his little house in Riverton was one of the first places the sheriff searched. He didn't find a thing. Not a hair. Not a fingerprint. Nothing."

Because Nicole had been held in the secret room under Fiona's barn. Trapped without sunlight. Then stuffed in the trunk of a car. Fiona suppressed a shudder. "I want to thank you again, Carolyn, for letting Belinda drop Mickey off here."

"It's what Nicole would have done."

The two children burst into the dining room with Jesse following.

"Mommy," Abby said, "may we please, please, please have a cookie before dinner?"

"Pleeeeeeze," Mickey said.

"Do you promise to eat all your veggies at dinner?"

"Yes, yes, yes."

"One cookie apiece." She lifted her gaze to Jesse's face. "And you can have one, too."

"Last time I checked," he said, "you weren't my mother."

A good thing. Because the thoughts she had whenever he came near to her were anything but motherly. The cell phone in her pocket rang, and she answered.

It was Belinda. Her voice was tense. "Fiona, I need to talk to you. I didn't want to say anything in front of Dylan and Carolyn. But I can tell you."

Leaving the Carlisle house right now was inconvenient to say the least. And Fiona didn't feel right about dumping the kids with Carolyn. "Can it wait until you come to pick up Mickey?"

"I don't know. I suppose so." Her tone was diffident. "I'm probably making too much of this."

"Wait." Fiona had a sense of urgency. As a rule, Belinda was down-to-earth, steady and stable. She wouldn't have called if it wasn't important. "What's wrong? What is it?"

"Nothing. Forget I called."

"I'll be there in twenty minutes."

When she disconnected the call, Jesse was watching her, patiently waiting for the piece of information that would make sense of everything else. "I need to run into town," she said.

"No problem," Carolyn said. "I'll go with you."

Belinda had specifically mentioned that she didn't want to talk in front of Dylan and Carolyn. "Actually—"

"I'll take her," Jesse said.

"Whoa, there." Fists on hips, Carolyn confronted them both. "Something's going on here, and I refuse to be left out of the loop."

"As soon as I know anything," Fiona said, "I'll call on your cell."

"I want to be there."

Her mother gave Carolyn a hug. "Of course, you want to be there. As soon as you learned how to walk, you insisted on leading the pack. That's why you're a terrific CEO."

"Thanks, Mom."

"But Fiona can handle this. She's quite capable. And she has Jesse to protect her." She pointed them toward the door. "Go."

MINUTES LATER, Jesse was behind the wheel of the Longbridge Security SUV, driving toward

Riverton. "Did Belinda tell you what was bothering her?"

"She didn't want to talk in front of Carolyn or Dylan."

He remembered how Mickey's mother had quailed in the presence of the Carlisles. "Making a good impression on them is important to her."

"Understandable. Her boyfriend works at the meatpacking plant in Delta, and his livelihood pretty much depends on the Carlisle Ranch." Though her seat belt was fastened, she reached toward him. Her fingers traced the Longbridge Security patch on his jacket. "She sounded scared."

He was already on high alert with adrenaline pumping through his veins. The end of their investigation was near. Like any good hunter, he sensed the nearness of his prey.

And he didn't like the idea of having Fiona with him at this moment, would have felt better if she'd stayed behind at the house where half a dozen guards could be watching. "We need to be careful. Stay close to me. Do as I say."

"I can't imagine that Richter is going to attack me in town. Not with all these witnesses."

He parked on Riverton's main street in front of the café. Though it was only a few minutes after four o'clock—too early for the dinner rush—several other cars were pulled up at the curb. It was the edge of sunset, beginning to get dark.

Inside, the café was decorated for Christmas with red and green ribbons and plastic Santas. Jesse scanned from the booths along the wall to the countertop, counting a total of twelve customers—cowboys, teenagers and a young couple, holding hands across the tabletop.

As soon as Belinda saw them, she led them through the kitchen into the area behind the café. The alley was bordered by a weathered fence that separated the restaurant from a two-story brick building that looked as though it had been built a hundred years ago. A row of metal garbage cans lined the wall behind the kitchen. In summer, there would have been flies and a stink. At this time of year, it was only an eyesore.

Belinda pulled Fiona into a hug. "Thank you for coming. I didn't know what to do."

Fiona comforted her, patting her shoulder and murmuring about how there was nothing to be afraid of. As Jesse watched, he marveled at Fiona's patience with her friend's nervous chatter. Though he was capable of waiting for hours as a hunter, he was already irritated by Belinda's tears.

With a visible effort, she pulled herself together. Using a napkin from the café, she swabbed at the smeared mascara under her eyes. "I heard you talking about a car that somebody had bought recently and how it had something to do with the kidnapping."

"That's right," Fiona said encouragingly.

"Nate bought a car." Her lips tightened. "He

told me about it when we were at the Circle M. He said if I needed a car this winter, he had one for me."

Jesse wasn't too impressed with this vague bit of information. "Did he mention Zeke O'Toole?"

She shook her head. "Definitely not. I would have remembered. I just thought Nate was bragging, pumping himself up now that he's left his little house in town and moved back to the Circle M."

Jesse recalled his brief search at Nate's ranch. He should have gone deeper, but the place had been thoroughly scrutinized the day before by both the sheriff and the FBI. Those searches had taken place before Nate moved back. *Before.*

"Thanks for the information," he said to Belinda. "We'll be sure to have somebody check it out."

"I'm so ashamed that I married him." Her lip quivered. "I was young, only nineteen. But that's no excuse."

Fiona patted her shoulder. "You have your own life, your own identity. Nobody judges you because of Nate."

"Did you see the way Dylan looked at me? Like I was dirt under his feet."

"He's upset," Fiona said.

Jesse added, "His family has been feuding with the Millers for years."

"It's not personal," Fiona said. "He doesn't hate you."

"Not yet." Belinda sighed. "There's something else I have to tell you. It's about that photo on the computer. The picture of Nicole after she'd been kidnapped."

"What about it?" he asked.

"She was wearing my blouse. I threw it away a couple of years ago when I left Nate, but I recognized the print. The cardigan, too. They both were mine. And that sheet hanging behind her? I had sheets that same color when I was living with Nate."

A surge went through Jesse. This was the information he'd been waiting for. Everything would now make sense.

He clarified, "You threw those clothes away."

"I never liked the shirt. Nate bought it for me, and he must have pulled it out of the trash." Belinda shuddered. "When I left him, he took it hard. He was watching me and Mickey all the time. Like a stalker."

"That's when you moved into Fiona's place."

"Living there saved my life." She took Fiona's hand and squeezed. "It gave me some physical distance from Nate. He stopped bothering me."

And Jesse knew why. With his handyman skills, Nate had constructed that secret room under the barn where he could hide out and keep an eye on Belinda and his son, watching them every minute. Like a classic stalker, he'd saved her clothing.

And when the time came, he had a ready hiding place for Nicole.

Though Nicole had been initially kidnapped by Richter, Nate had taken her from him. He was the third man. The man who picked up the ransom.

While keeping a watchful eye on the two women, Jesse took a step back. "I need to make a phone call."

He reached Burke, who was with the sheriff, inspecting Zeke O'Toole's car. Jesse was succinct. "Nate Miller is the kidnapper. He's the third man."

Chapter Twenty-Two

Fiona heard the urgency in Jesse's voice as he talked on the phone. Strategies were being planned. The kidnapping was on the verge of wrapping up.

She turned to Belinda. "You should take off work. Go to the ranch and pick up Mickey."

"What's happening?"

"You need to be with your son."

Belinda chewed her lower lip. "Are we in danger?"

It was entirely possible. No telling what

Nate would do when confronted. He might go after his ex-wife and child. "It might be best if you stay at the ranch until we get there."

"I never should have said anything."

"Don't think that. Not for a minute." As Fiona stared into her friend's eyes, she saw a reflection of her former self when she was timid and frightened by voices in the night. "You did the right thing, and you should be proud of yourself. Now go take care of your son."

As Belinda retreated into the kitchen of the café, Jesse motioned to Fiona. He closed his cell. "Burke, Dylan and the sheriff are on their way to the Circle M to arrest Nate."

"Do you need to be there?"

"They've got it covered. They aren't far from the Circle M. Burke is trying to set up some kind of strategy, but Dylan is dead set on charging straight ahead. Can't say as I blame him."

They walked through the alley behind the café to the sidewalk. The sun dipped behind the mountains; daylight faded to a murky gray. "You were right about being patient, Jesse. All we needed was the right bit of information. Now everything makes sense."

"Nate called the shots. He told Richter and Butch what to do and where to go." He frowned. "I'm still not sure why he set up such elaborate plans to arrange the meeting between Nicole and Dylan."

"I understand why." The emotional component to the kidnapping was the most obvious to her. "Nate despises Dylan. He wanted his enemy to suffer the same way he suffered when Belinda left him. He's obsessed with his hatred for the Carlisles."

When they rounded the corner onto Main Street, she noticed Jesse glancing left and right, still on the lookout for danger. She knew that he wouldn't take her hand while they were walking because he needed to be ready in case of an attack.

"I saw how crazy Nate was when we were at the Circle M," he said. "I should have—"

"Don't say it."

"What?"

"Don't blame yourself," she said firmly. "Nate has been suspicious from the start. But he's crafty, and he knows how to fly under the radar. The man built a secret room in my barn, and I didn't even know about it."

"The main thing is that we've got him," Jesse said. "This will be over soon."

Then what? After the danger passed, she would have no more need for a bodyguard. "Will you be moving on to another assignment?"

The question hung between them—a question that should have been asked the first moment she felt herself being attracted to him. Would he leave her?

Instead of answering, he hurried her toward the SUV.

A crisp mountain wind tossed the ribbons on

Christmas garlands wrapped around the light poles. Pedestrians in jackets and cowboy hats hurried along the sidewalk. A handful of cars and trucks with headlights lit pulled up to the four-way stop in Riverton's version of rush hour.

This little town hadn't changed too much over the years, and the easygoing pace suited her just fine. She didn't need to go faster. At this moment, she wished time would slow down or stop entirely. She didn't want to start counting the minutes until they had to say goodbye.

He held the passenger door open for her. She paused before slipping inside. "I don't want you to leave."

"Until Richter is in custody, I won't—"

"This isn't about Richter. Or Nate." She lifted her chin and looked up at him. "It's about you and me."

Now would be the perfect time for him to take her in his arms and kiss her and tell her that he wanted to be with her. Instead, he nudged her toward the seat. "We need to get going. I told Burke that while we were in town, we'd look in at Nate's old house. It's possible that he stashed the ransom there."

She slid onto her seat, and he closed the door. In her more timid and depressed days, Fiona would have thought that he was rejecting her. She would have given up without a fight.

But she knew that he cared for her. Damn it, their chemistry was undeniable. Hadn't he told her that he wanted to make love to her? Hadn't he said that he wanted their first night together to be special?

As she recalled, that conversation had ended badly, with Jesse talking about her lifestyle when she'd been the wife of Denver's district attorney. A lifestyle when she had everything she wanted. A lifestyle that no longer suited her.

When he slid behind the steering wheel, she said, "At least stay with me for tonight. I'll arrange for a babysitter. It'll be just you and me. I deserve that much. One night with you."

He fired up the engine. "That's not good enough."

Anger clenched around her heart. As he looked over his shoulder to back up, she yanked at the steering wheel. "We're not going anywhere until you explain yourself."

His mouth formed a hard, straight line, but he wasn't angry. Regret and pain registered in his eyes. "I want more than one night with you, Fiona. I want a lifetime. I want to be the love of your life. Your *only* love."

"Is this about Wyatt? About the fact that I was happily married before?"

"I can never be as right for you as he was. I can't compete with a ghost."

"Oh, Jesse." She wasn't sure whether to cry or laugh or knock him over the head. "Wyatt is a memory. You're real. Flesh and blood and one-hundred-percent real. You're the man I want beside me in bed."

"But you'll never stop thinking about Wyatt."

"I won't forget him." He had been a vital part of her life, the father of her child. "But that was a different time. A different place. I guess, I'm different now."

"Yes, you are."

"You saw it," she reminded him. "The way I'm changing."

"And I liked what I saw." Finally, he grinned. "I'm an ass."

"But a very, very sexy one."

"Promise me more than one night."

"As long as you want. I love you."

"I love you, Fiona." His voice was a smoky whisper. "We were meant to walk together through life. It's our path."

"A different path than either of us has ever walked before. Every step of the way is brand-new."

He kissed her, sealing their understanding, underlining the promise. "About tonight."

"We will be together," she promised. "Let's finish up here in town. Then we can get started on the rest of our life."

JESSE COULDN'T BELIEVE how neatly everything seemed to be falling into place. The kidnapping was almost solved. And, more important, he understood his relationship with Fiona. All it took was one simple word: *love*.

He hadn't been this happy in a long time. Maybe never. This was why he'd come back from death. To find her. To discover the possibility of a new life.

"I think you missed the turn," she said. "Again."

Riverton wasn't a big town, but he'd managed to get lost twice on the way to Nate's house. "I must be distracted."

"In a good way?"

"Very good."

He doubled back and found the right road at

the edge of town. Along this dead-end street, the small houses were set wide apart. Three in a row appeared to be vacant.

"This one." She pointed.

The one-story cottage had a peaked roof, but the square footage was hardly bigger than a trailer. There was a small barn and empty corral beside it. Lights shone from the house on the opposite side of the street where a truck was parked at the curb, but Nate's house was dark.

Jesse's cell phone rang. It was Burke.

He answered quickly. "What happened?"

"We found her." Burke's voice was jubilant. "We've got her. Nicole's okay."

"The ransom?"

"Not located yet."

"What about Nate?"

"We're still looking for him. Got to go. See you back at the ranch."

Jesse clicked his phone closed and gave Fiona the good news.

With a joyful whoop, she threw off her seat belt and climbed onto his lap. In the space of one minute, she must have kissed him sixty times. She was crazy-happy. Impulsive. Intuitive. Beautiful. Damn, he loved this woman.

"But no ransom," he said.

She jumped off his lap and opened her car door. "Maybe we'll find it inside."

In her excitement, she'd forgotten the standard security procedures he'd lectured her about. As he watched her dash toward the dark, little house, a sense of foreboding rose up inside him. He drew his weapon. "Fiona, wait!"

She halted and turned. The dim glow of a streetlight on the corner illuminated her features. Her beautiful face.

He strode toward her. "You need to do what I say."

Instead of arguing, she nodded. "I got a little carried away."

He was tempted to bundle her into the car and

drive away. *Let somebody else search Nate's house.* But the ransom hadn't yet been found. It was his job to follow every lead.

He walked beside her on the packed-earth driveway.

"How are we going to get inside?" she asked.

It'd be easy enough to break a window or pick the door lock. When he prowled around to the rear of the house, he discovered that neither procedure was necessary. The back door had been kicked open. "Somebody got here before us."

"Richter," she said.

And he could be inside the house. Time to call for backup.

Before Jesse could pull his cell phone from his pocket, he heard a sound. It came from overhead.

He looked up. Saw the glint of a weapon. A man crouched on the slanted roof.

He grabbed Fiona and threw her toward the house. She'd be hidden under the eaves.

Gunfire exploded. Four shots.

It seemed impossible that the gunman had missed. They were less than twenty yards apart. *It's not my time to die. I have too much to live for.*

Without taking aim, he returned fire. He dodged to the left, tried to get a better angle.

Heavy shadows hid the shooter as he scrambled up the incline toward the peak of the roof. His outline seemed misshapen, like a hunchbacked gargoyle.

Jesse fired again. He heard a groan.

The man on the roof stumbled. His gun clattered down from the eaves and hit the dirt in front of where Fiona was standing. She darted out from her hiding place and picked up the weapon.

"Give it up," Jesse called up to the man on the roof. "You haven't got a chance."

"I should have killed you the first time."

It was Richter, that son of a bitch. "Raise your hands."

He did exactly that. Jesse saw him clearly. He

wore a mountaineering backpack. *The ransom.* In his right fist, Richter held a hand ax.

Time stood still.

Everything went into slow motion.

Jesse saw Richter draw back his arm. The ax hurled toward him, flipping end over end. The blade aimed at his chest, directly at his heart.

He heard Fiona scream.

Jesse hit the dirt.

The effort of flinging the ax threw Richter off balance. He slid down the roof, crashed to the ground.

Jesse leaped to his feet, but Fiona got there first. She stood over the man who had terrorized her with her weapon pointed in his face.

She growled, "Don't move or I'll shoot."

Jesse believed her. Gentle, sweet Fiona had changed a lot in three days.

LATER THAT NIGHT, Fiona stepped through the door to her bedroom. Her hair was brushed to a sheen and she wore her best peignoir of pale blue satin. Jesse was already in her bed. The light of a dozen candles cast enticing shadows on his bared chest.

Abby was spending the night with Andrea at the Carlisle Ranch. There were no bodyguards or ranch hands circling the perimeter of her property. Finally, she and Jesse were alone.

She walked slowly toward the bed. The satin swished around her hips. Almost everything had worked out perfectly. Nicole was exhausted but unhurt. Richter was in police custody. In his backpack was most of the ransom money. They'd found Zeke O'Toole, tied up and scared but still alive. Nate Miller, unfortunately, was still at large.

She sat on the bed and drew a line down the center of Jesse's chest. "When I saw that ax flying through the air toward you, I thought it was over."

"No way would I die before tonight." His grin

was slow and sexy. "I had to outsmart death. To get to you."

"This is where you're meant to be."

He pulled her close. "With you, Fiona. Forever."

* * * * *